The Trouble with
Terry

The Trouble with Terry

by JOAN LEXAU

Illustrated by Irene Murray

SCHOLASTIC BOOK SERVICES

NEW YORK · TORONTO · LONDON · AUCKLAND · SYDNEY · TOKYO

Although this story and the people in it are fictitious, there was once a gang of children and parents. To the "old gang" and to the other neighbors, this book is dedicated.

CONTENTS

F Is for Finally

"No more pencils, no more books, no more teacher's dirty looks!"

All the children but one were chanting it as they leaped, ran, and danced out of the school building. It was Friday noon and the start of summer vacation. One second they were still in school, the next, one more step, and they were free — or would be when they crossed the street.

The police boys were having trouble making the lines re-form on the sidewalk. Finally they were ready, and still chanting, they shuffled off to the corner.

The only quiet one was Teresa Seth, 10 years old, with an F in arithmetic on her report card.

Terry kept in step with her fifth-grade class, her

books, pencil box, ruler, and notebooks in her arms, and stared unseeing at the feet of the girl ahead of her.

At last they were at the corner and crossing the street. Each one, on reaching the opposite curb, gave a glad whoop and raced down the sidewalk.

When Terry reached the other side, she went on walking as before. Her classmates were soon ahead of her.

"Terry, c'mon, hurry up," Cindy Ford called back to her. She waited for Terry to catch up.

Terry and Cindy had once been best friends even though they lived two and a half blocks apart. Then another girl, Kimberly Schaeffer, had moved in a couple of houses away from Cindy, and the two played together all the time. Whenever Terry came along, they were always in the middle of something. They seemed glad to see her, but still she felt left over. She seldom went to play with Cindy now.

Kim said, "Gee, Terry, you look like it's the end of the world. Doesn't she, Cindy?"

"I saw the F on your report card," Cindy said. "I couldn't help it. I don't know why they have to write them in red anyhow."

"You shouldn't feel so bad about it," Kim said. "I've had a couple of F's in spelling. My folks hardly even rant and rave about it anymore." She stopped, seeing by Terry's expression that this was the wrong thing to say.

Terry didn't know how she was going to tell her

mother. Her mother often said, "One thing I don't have to worry about. My children get good marks in school. Not that they couldn't do still better," she'd add, looking at Terry. Her brother Tommy couldn't do much better if he tried. He was a year and a half older than Terry and about five years brainier, she thought bitterly.

"If I'd only had some idea," she said. "Mrs. Selby said when she held me back at recess that she'd tried to warn me."

The girls were walking down the block, pausing now and then to get a better grip on their books.

"Anyhow," Terry said, kicking at a stone, "Mrs. Selby may be nice but she doesn't mark fair."

"What do you mean?" Kim said, surprised. "I thought she was fair."

"Lots of times she isn't," Terry insisted. "Like the time it said in a test that somebody spent twenty-five cents one day, and seventy-five cents the next day, and fifty cents the day after. And just because she'd been telling us about averages, she wanted us to say it was the same as spending fifty cents each day. But you can't buy something for seventy-five cents if you only spend fifty cents so I said it was the same as spending what was spent, and she marked it wrong."

"Gee, I never thought of that," Kim said.

"Did you talk to Mrs. Selby about it?" Cindy wanted to know.

"What good would it do?" Terry said. "I talked to

her the time she asked what kind of lines didn't meet, and she wouldn't change my mark."

"What kind of lines did you say?" Cindy asked.

"I said faraway lines. And Mrs. Selby said it should have been parallel lines. But remember when she said railroad tracks were parallel lines? And railroad tracks meet. You look at any picture of railroad tracks and you'll see. Mrs. Selby said they only seem to meet and if you walked up to where you saw them meet, you'd see they didn't. But they *do* meet from where you're standing in the first place. I tried to tell her, but she wouldn't listen." Terry was almost in tears at the injustice of it.

"You'd think she'd have marked you half-right anyhow," Kim said.

Terry took a deep breath to keep from crying and went on, "And I talked to her about the multiplication tables too. I asked her why we had to remember them when we could write them down in a notebook and look them up when we needed them. She asked if I wanted to carry a notebook around the rest of my life, and I said I wouldn't mind. I really wouldn't. But she wouldn't let me do it that way."

"I think teachers are like parents," Kim said. "They listen to you but they never agree with you. Even when you're right."

They had reached Kim's house. She went in to eat, calling over her shoulder, "See you in a little while, Cindy. You, too, Terry. You come back and play."

"Why don't you stay and have lunch with me, Terry?" Cindy said. "You could ride my bike."

The only fight they'd had when they were best friends had been over Cindy's bike. The day Cindy got it, she had taught Terry how to ride it. For Terry, it was like being in heaven. After that, every time she came to Cindy's house, her first words had been, "Can I ride your bike?"

Until one day Cindy exploded, "Do you come to see me or my bike?"

Now all Terry said was, "I want to get this junk home." She didn't feel much like playing, or even bike riding.

She walked slowly home. At the end of Cindy's street the houses stopped. From there on, down a block and over a block, all was woods. On the corner after the woods was Terry's apartment house.

One day Terry had overheard somebody walking by say that it looked like a crackerbox. She'd burned at the tone of it, but she had to admit that the building did look like a huge, red-brick crackerbox. It was four stories high, four windows wide in front and back, and ten windows wide at each side. All the apartments had two rooms, and they were all exactly alike except for the furniture. Terry lived with her mother and brother in the third-floor front apartment, that had side windows facing the woods.

Her brother was just coming out the front door when Terry reached it. He had already changed to

11

his play clothes and was munching on a peanut butter sandwich.

His friend Danny was waiting out in front and Danny's older brother Mike was crashing down the stairs, with their five-year-old brother Soupy calling behind them, "Wait for me, wait for me."

"Hey, what'd you get?" Tommy asked her. "I got all A's. Except for art and that doesn't count."

Terry shrugged. She wasn't going to yell it out before the others.

"What's the matter, you have a fight with somebody or something?" he asked, noticing how miserable she looked.

She shook her head.

Tommy said to the others, "You guys go over and start, and I'll be over in a couple of minutes." He followed Terry up the stairs. "Something's the matter," he said. "What happened?"

When they were in the apartment, she threw her books on the sofa and took the report card out of her pencil box and showed it to him.

Her brother took a long look at the card. And then he looked again to make sure he wasn't seeing things.

"Must be a mistake," he said. "It's always been your worst subject, but you never even got a D before, did you?" He looked at the year's line of marks. "Nothing below a C minus. Got to be a mistake."

"No it isn't," Terry said. "She told me about it ahead of time, during recess. She said I improved in everything else, but during arithmetic all I do lately is stare

out the window. And my arithmetic homework's gotten abdominal."

"Gotten *what?*" Tommy yelled.

"Abdominal. That means it's a mess."

Tommy hooted. "You mean abominable. What do you use big words for if you can't say them right?"

Terry flushed. If he knew what she meant, why did he have to make fun of her?

"Say, what are you going to tell Mom about your report card?" Tommy asked.

Terry shook her head. "I don't know. How mad do you think she'll be?"

"Who knows? You want me to tell her? You can stay outside till it's over," he offered.

"No. Last time we did that, remember, she caught on and only got madder than ever." Terry threw her books in an angry heap behind the sofa.

Tommy jumped as if he'd been hit. "What d'you think you're doing with those books?" he yelled. "My gosh, the way you treat books I'm surprised they let you take any out of the library."

He reached back of the couch and picked up one of her books. "Look at this. Ink and pencil marks all over it, pages bent. When I got through with this, it was just as good as when I got it. Boy, I hate to see you get hold of my books."

"What do you care? They aren't your books any more. And I only do it with the crummy schoolbooks," Terry retorted.

Tommy started for the door. "Just the same, no book should be treated that way." Before he went out, he added in a milder tone, "We'll be over in the woods playing hide and seek, case you want to come."

Terry was left alone with her misery. She huddled in a lump on the sofa and thought about all the reasons she had to be sorry for herself.

In the first place, she was always being scolded for something. Practically every minute. She wondered if there had ever been a day when she hadn't been yelled at at least a hundred times. This year, since she had stopped playing with Cindy so much, it seemed that the scoldings had grown worse.

And then she had to be born a girl. That wasn't fair at all. Girls couldn't play football, couldn't have paper routes, they were supposed to stay clean all the time and practically not even breathe, and certainly not have any fun.

Her mother acted like she'd *asked* to be a girl. "Why can't you be a young lady?" her mother kept saying. But why should she? And she was stuck with being a girl the rest of her life. It just wasn't right. If there had to be girls, they should be treated like anybody else.

To make life really impossible, she had to have a big brother. If it weren't for Tommy, maybe her mother wouldn't think she was such a mess. As it was, all she heard was, "Why can't you be neat, like your brother. Why can't you do what you're told right away, like your brother. How can you always lose things? Tommy never does. Tommy doesn't break everything he touches."

Tommy this, Tommy that. There were probably worse big brothers. Kim's brother was always snitching on her or hitting her. But Terry almost wished her brother was like that. Every time she got to really being mad at him, he'd do something nice that made it impossible.

Terry tried to make the tears come, but they wouldn't. They never did when she wanted them to. Not when she was alone and could cry in peace. No, she always had to burst out bawling when there were ten million people around.

She shoved the report card behind a sofa cushion so her mother wouldn't see it the first thing when she came in. There must be something she could do. If she did something ladylike, like housework, maybe her mother wouldn't be so mad.

What should she do? Dust? No, the last time she'd dusted, she'd knocked a picture off the wall. Her mother had been angry even though the glass hadn't broken.

"How can you knock a picture off the wall dusting the dresser?" her mother had yelled.

It wouldn't have done any good if Terry had explained she was pretending the hand with the dustcloth was a plane, landing and taking off on the dresser top. Her mother didn't understand things like that. To a grownup, it was wrong to try to get any fun out of housework.

Well, she wouldn't dust, but there must be something. Yes, there was something much better. She could scrub the linoleum in the living room. Her mother might even notice that without being told.

Terry got a rag and the soap and pail from the closet in Tommy's room and opened the doors to the kitchen part of the room. The water wasn't hot at this time of day, so she poured in a lot of soap.

Floor scrubbing wasn't so bad, Terry thought, as she swished the rag around. She was on a beach, and the tide was coming in. When the water lapped up too close to her knees, she moved further up the beach.

"Anchor's aweigh, my boys, anchor's a — weigh," she sang out heartily. "Farewell to college joys, WE SAIL AT BREAK OF DAY-DAY-DAY-DAY—"

Pound, pound, pound came from the ceiling.

"Blast that old Miss Jefferson," she muttered. She went on singing more quietly.

It wasn't long before she was working on the last corner. And look how that floor shone!

But — good heavens — she hadn't done that bit. And then she remembered. Her mother had waxed the floor Tuesday night. All Terry would have had to do to make it all shiny again was go over it with plain water. What she'd done was wash all the wax off.

Terry pounded the rag on the floor. "Blast — blast — blast!"

As soon as the floor dried, she'd have to wax it. Otherwise, her mother would notice the difference for sure. She wouldn't appreciate it either.

While she was waiting for the floor to dry, Terry read the instructions on the back of the wax can. "Wash floor," it said. Well, that was done.

Terry groaned aloud at the next words: "Rinse thoroughly." The instructions said to be sure that every bit of soap was removed. Oh, no! And all that soap she'd used.

Terry rinsed the floor once and let it dry. There was still a film of soap on it. Twice more she rinsed it before all the soap was off.

She wasn't on a beach anymore. Now she was in the middle of the ocean on a leaky raft. Her knees were sore and her back ached. And she was *never, never, never* going to grow up to be a lady and do housework all her life.

When she had finished the last rinsing, she got up and hobbled to a chair by the table in the other room. She was so tired, and so hot! Except for her knees where her dress had gotten soaked and was clinging to her. Her school dress! She'd forgotten to change to her jeans. Her mother would be furious.

As soon as the floor was dry, Terry changed clothes and buried her dress at the bottom of the dirty clothes pile.

In a blazing temper she unscrewed the top off the wax can and hurled the top at the floor. At the same moment, she dropped the can of wax. Wax oozed out.

"Oh, BILGE!" Terry shrieked.

Well, she'd just have to start waxing from this part of the room. Her temper soon cooled under the rhythmic movement of her hand as she covered the floor with wax. And it did look nice. Wherever she touched the rag, the floor took on a new look. Like King Midas turning things to gold.

She was nearly done when Tommy walked in.

"Did you have to come in now?" she yelled. "Couldn't you have waited till it dried?"

Tommy gaped at her. "What on earth are you doing?" he asked.

"Well, what does it look like I'm doing?" she snapped.

He was about to say he thought she hated housework, but he thought better of it. Instead, he said reasonably, "Look, how was I supposed to know? I only came in to get my paper bag. And to tell you that you could tell Mom it's my fault about the F. On account of my paper route, and our not doing our homework together any more to save me time."

"Oh," Terry said. "That's an idea." She didn't point out that doing their homework together had hurt her as much as helped. After Tommy checked her homework, he showed her his. He always made his seem like fun. She knew hers wasn't. So she ended up knowing more about decimals than fractions.

"Say, what are *you* going to do?" he asked. "About footprints," he added, as she looked at him blankly.

Terry looked around her. She had waxed herself into a corner. That figured. It just *figured*.

At least Tommy didn't laugh, although he looked like he wanted to. "I'll try not to make any more prints than I can help," he said. He took a flying leap to the doorway of his room, and just two leaps on the way out. "See you later," he called.

Terry looked around for a place to get off the floor. The only thing near enough was the radiator. That would have to do.

Sitting on the radiator, she finished the last bit of waxing by shoving the rag around with her foot. She looked again at the wax can. "Allow twenty minutes for drying," it said on the back.

Before one minute was up, Terry was squirming. What an uncomfortable place a radiator was. At the end of two minutes she couldn't stand it any more. She'd just have to rewax her footprints as well as Tommy's.

She walked over to the sofa and tried to think of something to do while she was waiting. Tommy's books must be behind the sofa, too. Yes, there was *Tales of Today and Yesterday*. She'd already read that when he was out on his paper route, and he'd never found out. Well, she'd see how many words she knew from next year's speller.

By the time the floor was dry, she decided that next year spelling would be as easy as ever. Very often she was the last one up in a spelling bee. It was because she read so much, she guessed.

Terry touched up the footprints and stood in the doorway to admire her work. She didn't think her mother could have done any better. Now if she could only think of some nice way to break the news of her report card to her mother.

When Mrs. Seth came home, Terry was asleep on the sofa. She jumped up as her mother came in.

"How can you sleep on a day like this?" her mother wondered. "The sun is shining and it's your first half-day of vacation."

Terry yawned. "Oh, cookies!" she said, seeing the bag in her mother's arm. "I forgot it was payday."

Her mother worked in a cookie factory. For twenty-five cents she could buy a huge bag of cookies that were broken or for some other reason weren't just right. Once a month she brought home cookies, and on the other payday they had ice cream.

"Not till after supper," her mother warned.

"O.K.," Terry said meekly.

Her mother looked at her sharply. "Teresa Seth, what have you got all over you? Look at your hands. And on your face and clothes, too. Honestly, you're more of a boy than your brother."

Terry looked at the dried wax on her hands. She couldn't think of anything to say. After all her work, all she got for it was a scolding. She had all she could do to keep from blubbering.

"You go take a shower," her mother said, "while I cook supper. And get into your other jeans and shirt."

Terry put on her rubber slippers, grabbed her

clothes and a towel and soap. She stamped down the hall to the shower room shared by all the families on the third floor.

She was so discouraged that she didn't even yell when she stubbed her toe coming out of the shower, nor did she take any pleasure in the squish-squish-squish of her rubber slippers as she went back to her apartment.

Her mother smiled at her as she came in. "There, doesn't that feel better?" she asked. "Supper's ready now. You can whistle Tommy in."

Terry took the whistle from its nail by the window and tooted twice. Each family had its own signal for whistling the children in.

Still Terry didn't know how she was going to tell her mother about her report card. Should she do it now, while her mother seemed to be in a good mood? But she couldn't bring herself to do it. And yet she knew she should bring it up before her mother remembered the report cards herself.

Supper was a quiet meal. Terry had nothing to say, her mother kept staring at her, and Tommy uneasily watched them both.

After supper Terry stacked the dishes. As her mother was washing them, she said, with her back to Terry, "Are you out of sorts because I scolded you?"

"No," Terry mumbled. And then, when her mother looked at her, "Well, I guess I was pretty dirty."

They both smiled at the same moment, and Terry knew she would never have a better time to tell her mother. Yet she didn't want to break the spell. After all her hours of worry, it was like the sun coming out after a rain, and she didn't want to make the sun go back behind a cloud. She hesitated, and the moment passed.

"You don't have to dry dishes tonight," her mother said. "The last day of school should be a special day. Just take the garbage down the hall, and then you can go out and play."

It was a special day, all right, Terry thought grimly, as she took the bag of garbage and went down the hall toward the garbage room. Oh, she could kick herself for not saying something when she had the chance!

She was so angry that she opened the door, shut her eyes, and hurled the bag as hard as she could toward the ceiling, even though she knew she'd have to pick it up to put it in one of the cans.

The bag hit the ceiling with a thud and Terry opened her eyes — and looked straight into the eyes of Mr. Bayard, who lived in the apartment next door to the garbage room.

It was too much! Mr. Bayard began to laugh, and Terry burst into tears and fled.

Mr. Bayard called after her, "Don't cry, Terry. It's all right."

"What on earth — " said her mother.

Terry went straight to the sofa and dug out her report card. The tears still streaming down her face, she handed the card to her mother, who had followed her into the living room.

Her mother read the card and then looked at her daughter while Terry fought down her sobs. There was a short silence, with Terry and Tommy hardly breathing.

Then her mother said, "Well, at last. I was beginning to think my children weren't normal. Finally one of you got an F."

Tommy laughed. "That's what the F's for — finally."

But their mother was staring at the floor. "Good heavens!" she said. "I can't believe it."

"Terry waxed it," Tommy said helpfully.

Terry wished he'd kept his big mouth shut. Now her mother would say, "But what on earth for? I just waxed it."

But instead her mother looked again at the report card and back at the floor. And Terry knew her mother understood exactly why she'd waxed the floor.

"You did a beautiful job," her mother said gently. "Thank you."

"That's all right," Terry said. She didn't know what else to say. She would have hugged her mother if they had been the hugging kind. Instead, she made a resolution to help her mother more often. Only next time she was going to think what she was doing first.

Her mother started back to the kitchen. "I don't know why I brought those cookies home. Nobody seems to want them," she said.

Terry and her brother ran for the cookie bag.

"First dibs on a chockly graham," Terry yelled.

"Kinders, feepers," Tommy said firmly.

Over the clinking of the dishes in the sink, Terry heard her mother saying, "Now if I could work out a deal with her teacher, maybe I wouldn't have to do any housework at all next year."

Terry and Tommy decided it was time they went outside before the street lights came on and they had to come in again.

There was a whole summer before them, Terry thought happily. A summerful of fun and excitement before school began again.

Down by the River

TERRY REACHED BACK and peeled the shirt from her skin for about the five hundredth time.

"If only it wasn't so bloody hot," she said. She'd been reading about the Bastables lately and was feeling very English.

"Oh, I say! Rawther!" Tommy replied instantly.

It was too hot even to point out to him how beastly he was. Terry looked at the others squatting on the curb beside her and wondered if they could possibly be as hot as she was. They were all there, Terry, Tommy, Mike, Danny, and Greg. Danny and Greg were eleven and in the same grade as Tommy, even though he was twelve. Tommy had been born the wrong time of year to be in the grade ahead with Mike.

Since lunch they'd been sitting and waiting until one of them thought of something to do. Something they hadn't already tired of in the week since vacation started.

Suddenly Mike burst out, "Dooby, dooby, dooby, dooby, doo." It sounded more like the tired downhill side of piano scales than a song.

"We could go to your house, Greg," Danny said.

It wasn't nice to invite yourself somewhere. But even so, Terry was glad Danny had said it. Greg's house would be cooler. Greg was the only one in the gang who didn't live in the apartment building. He lived on the same street, on the other side of the woods, and they often played there. His mother was home during the day and sometimes she made lemonade for them.

"Can't," Greg said. "My ma's got a sinus headache and she doesn't want me around more than necessary."

Just then Soupy started to cry again. He was trying to skate on some rusty skates and kept falling down. Every time he fell, he burst into tears. Terry could tell from the way he cried that the tears were from habit, not from hurt.

"There goes crybaby again," Mike said.

"Shut up, stupid," Danny told his little brother without even bothering to turn around.

Terry couldn't blame Mike and Danny too much for being impatient with Soupy. It seemed that he was always crying about something. In fact, that was why he was called Soupy when his real name was Kevin. Well, maybe she could do something about it.

Slowly and carefully Terry stood up. Her legs were all pins and needles from sitting in one position so long. She went over to Soupy and yanked him to his feet. Immediately he stopped crying and smiled at her.

"Listen, Soup, I want to tell you something," Terry said. "I used to be a crybaby myself."

"I'm not a crybaby," Soupy said.

"Yes, you are," Terry said, "but I'm going to help you stop. Look, you're going to be in first grade this year, and — "

"Going to be rich then," Soupy shouted, and got himself so excited that he nearly fell over again and Terry had to grab him. He and Danny and Mike were always talking about all the things they were going to do when Soupy was in school all day and their father got a regular job. Now their father visited factories, taking Soupy with him, and wrote articles for magazines about the machines and things. In between times he typed envelopes or whatever work he could get. But he had already been offered his old job back as a newspaper reporter for next fall.

"I know," Terry said, "but that's not what I mean. When I was in the first grade I still cried all the time, and you know what happened? In second grade I saw a note on the teacher's desk, a note the first-grade teacher had written about everybody. And after my name it said, 'Cries easily.' It was awful, Soupy, all written down like that, and you don't want that to happen to you, do you?"

Before Soupy had a chance to say he didn't care, Terry went on, "I'll tell you what to do. When you fall, instead of crying, just say to yourself, 'So I fell. So what?' And then get up and don't think about it anymore."

"O.K.," Soupy said.

"Well, try it," Terry said. "Go ahead and fall."

"Now?" Soupy asked.

"Sure," said Terry.

Soupy fell down so hard that Terry flinched. He didn't make a sound, just sat there blinking at her.

"See?" Terry said. "What did I tell you. It works."

Soupy went on sitting and staring. "What did you say I should say to myself?" he asked.

"Oh, Soupy, you're hopeless!" Terry sighed. But then she remembered that, after all, he hadn't cried. "I tell you what," she told him. "If you'll stop crying all the time, I'll take you to the library and you can take out a book on my card. Just one, though, because I can only take out four at a time." Soupy had been begging her to take him to the library for a long time. Several times she had taken out a book to read to him, even though it was embarrassing. She hoped the librarian knew those books weren't for herself.

A woman walking by smiled at Soupy and he gave her an angelic smile in return. Then he got to his feet and wobbled after her.

"Soupy, you come back here," Terry yelled. She had cured him of asking the women who went by if they were his mother, but he still followed them sometimes. His own mother had spent all the money they had and more besides and then just went away one day when Soupy was a baby. She left a lot of bills and a note saying she was sorry but probably they could get along better without her. Soupy had been told his mother was sick and went away to get well. She must have been sick, Terry thought, to do a thing like that. Terry's father had died so long ago that all she remembered about him was his mustache. But which was worse, she wondered, to have a parent die or go away and leave you?

She had to run and drag Soupy back. And then, to show him he'd been bad, she went to the curb and sat down, just in time to hear Mike say, "We could ride up to the pool and go swimming."

Terry wanted to cry out No, but she held it back. If they went swimming, that meant she couldn't go along. Tommy would go with Greg on Greg's bike, and Danny and Mike on their bike. If Terry walked, by the time she got there they'd be starting for home.

And they wouldn't *care*, not one of them. Well, maybe Tommy would a little, but not enough to stop him from going. None of the boys complained about her being in the gang, but they didn't miss her when she wasn't there, she was sure. When they played baseball, Tommy was the only one who remembered when it was her turn at bat.

Tommy said now, "I wish we'd thought of that earlier. If we started out now, I wouldn't get back in time for my route."

"Yeah," Danny said, "and all those hills. It's my turn to pedal and I don't think I could make those hills today."

"Hey, I know what!" Tommy said. "Let's go down by the river. That should be cool."

That seemed like a good idea to all of them and they started out right away. There was a furious sound of clumping skates behind them.

Danny yelled, "You stay home, Soupy. You can't come where we're going."

"Go on back, Soupy," Mike said when Soupy kept coming. "Do as I say or I'll give you a swat."

Soupy stopped but he was looking at Terry as though she were a criminal. She felt sorry for him and ran back. "We won't be gone long," she said. "I wish you could come, too, but you'd fall if you tried to climb down the bank. We don't want you to get hurt, Soupy."

Soupy turned away and wouldn't answer. Terry gave up and ran to catch up with the others. At least he hadn't cried. Maybe she had taught him something.

The Mississippi River was six blocks away. They went to their special place, marked by a tall, broad-limbed tree. By the tree was a path leading to a rock ledge, hanging out high and scary over the river. Beside the ledge it was possible to go down all the way to the river itself. Even though the bank was steep, the boys raced down. Terry thumped down on the seat of her jeans. It was clumsy but safe.

When she got to the bottom, the boys were already roaming the shore of the inlet looking for treasure. Once they had found a rubber doll, so faded and flattened that even Terry didn't want it. Today they didn't find anything. Terry breathed in the river smell, old and stale, yet fresh and exciting at the same time.

"Hey, look at the bottom part of the bridge," Mike yelled. "I never noticed before, it must go all the way across the river like that."

They all stared at it. The under part of the bridge looked like huge white waves of concrete. It started on the shore they were on and continued uphill and down, all the way across, as far as they could see.

Mike ran to the bridge and up to the top of the first wave. "Last one across is a rickety rocket," he yelled as he turned and disappeared on the other side of the wave.

In a flash the other boys were on the bridge and running. Terry followed more slowly, half crawling up the incline. She didn't like this at all. The bridge was wide enough, but the hills were steep and, except at the top of each hill, there was nothing at the sides. Just the edge and then the river down below. What would happen, Terry worried, if they were caught on this part of the bridge? But it wasn't likely that anyone would see them, unless a barge came by. Anyhow, she didn't want to be left by herself, so she kept on doggedly.

On the top of the first crest, Terry slouched over to keep from hitting the top part of the bridge and looked ahead. She could see Greg on the next crest and Tommy halfway up it, with Mike on the one beyond them. Mike was sitting down, resting. She could see him panting. Danny was out of sight. Terry slid cautiously down her hill, torn between going on and going back.

Just as she reached the bottom, she heard a chortling noise behind her. There was Soupy, standing at the top of the rise, still on his roller skates. He had followed them somehow without making enough noise for them to hear. He must have crawled up the concrete. And there he was, eyes closed, laughing at the trick he'd played. All of a sudden his skates began to take him downhill, toward the edge of the bridge.

At first Terry was so terrified, she couldn't move. She heard herself screaming, "SOUPY!" and that woke her up. Without thinking, she dashed up the hill and threw herself at Soupy, knocking him safely aside. But she was right at the edge and her momentum carried her on. She felt her legs go over the side. And then she was digging into the concrete with her elbows and her hands.

She could hear Tommy yelling, "Hold on, Terry, we're coming, *hold on.*" His voice sounded far away.

"Please God, make them hurry," Terry prayed. "I can't hold on much longer." Her shoulders were burning with pain.

"You pushed me down," an aggrieved voice said

in her ear. And then in alarm, "You won't fall down, Terry, will you?" Two small hands pulled at her hair and the back of her shirt. Soupy was crying now in earnest.

With the last of her breath, Terry managed to say clearly, "You can't pull me up, Soupy. Go away from the edge. I mean it." Her arms gave way.

But she was going up instead of down. Strong hands were pulling her from every direction, wherever they could get hold. Slowly she was dragged up onto the bridge.

Nobody said anything for a while. They were all too winded and dazed. Terry lay still, gazing at the sky. It was a beautiful sky, and the soft clouds fluttering across it were beautiful too. Finally she sat up and looked around her.

Soupy smiled and started up to come over to her. Danny pulled him down. "You stay put, meathead," he said. "Of all the idiotic things to do, following us down here."

"Everybody pushes me," Soupy howled. "Terry *promised* she'd take me to the liberary and she dint. She went away, and she *promised*."

Terry remembered she had said she'd take him to the library if he didn't cry all the time. "But I didn't mean right away, Soupy," she cried. That must have been why he was so angry when she left him. And why he had come after her to the river.

Mike shook his finger in Soupy's face and said, "That's enough out of you. You just ought to be glad you're here. If Terry hadn't saved your life, you wouldn't be. If she'd gotten drowned in the river, it would have been your fault because you didn't mind when we told you to stay home. You remember that, next time we tell you to do something, *you under-stand?*"

Soupy nodded, his eyes wide with wonder. But he doesn't understand at all, Terry thought. He's too little.

"Must be about time for me to pick up my papers," Tommy said after a while. "You all right, Terry?"

"Sure," Terry said, jumping to her feet. Her legs collapsed and she fell down again. Laughing shakily, Terry got up more slowly, with Tommy and Greg's help. They held her until her legs were firm.

"Boy, are you a mess," Tommy said.

Terry was surprised to find that her arms and knees were torn and bloody. Now that she noticed them, they began to sting. Her shoulders still ached.

As soon as they were home, Terry went to get cleaned up. After asking her again if she was all right, Tommy went to pick up his papers.

Terry washed her arms and legs and got into jeans and a long-sleeved blouse. It was a good thing she'd worn shorts, she thought, because she might have torn her jeans and then she really would have caught it. But it was going to be pretty uncomfortable wearing long sleeves in this hot weather. She wondered if her mother would notice. None of the parents knew they played by the river. Terry suspected her mother would be angry if she found out.

It would still be a while before her mother came home. Terry settled down with one of her library books. Right away she liked Helen, the girl in the story. Helen was always doing things wrong too.

The book was Terry's favorite kind, both happy and sad, and she was completely absorbed in it when the silence was shattered by a voice saying, "What's the matter with you?" Her mother was standing over her.

"Wh-what?" Terry stammered.

"I've been talking to you for five minutes," her mother said impatiently. "You're pale. I hope you're not coming down with something."

"I feel O.K.," Terry said. Except for hurting all over, she added to herself.

"I suppose you've been in all day, reading," Mrs. Seth said.

"I'll go out right after supper," Terry said earnestly.

"After the dishes are done, you mean," her mother said, smiling a little, and she started toward the kitchen. There was a knock at the door and she answered it.

"Is Terry home?" Soupy's father asked. He and Soupy came in.

"What's all this about your saving Kevin's life?" Mr. O'Halloran asked Terry. "That's all he'll tell me, that Mike said that you had saved his life. And I can't find Mike and Danny, as usual. What happened?"

"I dint tell where," Soupy said proudly. "Mike told me not to."

Terry wished she could shake him. "Well," she began, thinking desperately, "you see, it looked like Soupy, I mean Kevin, was going to fall down. And so I, uh — I stopped him," she finished brightly.

"You pushed me down," Soupy said, gently.

"There's more to it than that," Terry's mother said. "I knew there was something as soon as I walked in the door. Now you tell me what happened, Terry, and you tell it right. I know you don't lie, but the way you walk around the truth sometimes, I'd think you'd get worn out."

Terry blushed. She knew she'd have to give part of it away. "Well, Soupy and I were down by the river. And he almost fell in. So I just stopped him. I mean, anybody would of," she said, not daring to look at anyone. At least she hadn't given away the others.

"You took Soupy down to the river?" her mother said in horror. "Are you out of your mind?"

"I followed her," Soupy said gayly. "And she dint see me. Nobody seen me. I went real quiet."

"Just what were you doing down by the river?" Mrs. Seth demanded. "And how long have you been going there? You knew I wouldn't want you playing there, Terry, didn't you? Was Tommy there too?"

"Everybody was there," Soupy said. "They said I couldn't go, but I *did*." Soupy was chortling with joy again just the way he was on the bridge.

"Well, Terry and Tommy won't be going there any more," their mother said.

"Oh, now, Mrs. Seth — " Soupy's father hesitated.

He looked embarrassed. "I don't want to interfere. But you might consider geography, for instance."

"Geography?" Mrs. Seth repeated.

"Yes. All over the country children have to learn about the location of the Mississippi River. And history — why, De Soto was buried in it, La Salle died trying to get to the mouth of the river, and — " Mr. O'Halloran took a breath and stopped. He was always saying that he was going to write a book on Midwestern history if he ever got the time. "Sorry," he said. "Didn't mean to make a speech."

Terry's mother smiled. "Don't be sorry," she said. "I'm glad you spoke up. Anyway, just the exercise of climbing up and down the riverbank should be good for a boy."

For a boy! Terry's sudden hope faded away.

"I want to thank you, Terry, for saving Kevin's life," Mr. O'Halloran said, his face reddening. Thanking people didn't come easy to him. "And for all that you've done for him all these years. I don't know what we'd do without you." His tone changed abruptly as he said, "Come on home, Kevin. You have a spanking coming for being disobedient. You're too young to go down to the river, but old enough to mind."

"Oh, please, don't spank him," Terry pleaded. Mike and Danny bragged about how hard their father hit them, and Terry couldn't bear the thought of it happening to Soupy. She told his father about the promise Soupy thought she'd broken.

"Well, I guess at Kevin's age you don't think be-

yond right this minute. He does get things awfully
mixed up sometimes. But I have to teach him to obey,
Terry. I tell you what, though. You can come along
and watch, and if you think I'm spanking him too
hard, just say so and I'll stop." Mr. O'Halloran was
grinning about something. Terry couldn't see anything funny.

Terry's mother said she could go if she came right
back. "I want to talk to you," she said ominously.

Soupy's father set out two chairs a little apart.
Terry thought maybe one was for her, but he didn't
say anything about it. So she stood and watched.

Mr. O'Halloran brought out a wicked looking belt
from the closet. "O.K., Kevin," he said. Soupy
sprawled out on his father's lap.

Still grinning, Soupy's father gave Soupy a little
pat on his rear. At the same moment he brought
the belt down with a hard *thwack* on the other chair.

"Ow!" Soupy yelled. *Thwack.* "Ow!" *Thwack.*
"Ow!" *Thwack.* "Ow!"

"Think you can do what you're told now?" his
father asked sternly.

"Ye-es," Soupy gasped. He stood up. "I dint cry,"
he announced. "I'm too big to cry allatime."

"That's wonderful, Soupy," Terry told him, trying
hard to keep a straight face.

"Anyhow, it dint hurt too much," he said.

"Hmmm," said his father. "Maybe next time it will
hurt a little more."

Terry went smiling down the hall. Her smile faded quickly when she reached her apartment.

"Now you can tell me exactly what happened at the river," her mother said sternly. "All of it. You weren't going to say anything at all about it, were you?"

Terry shook her head.

"And after you finish, you're going to promise me you won't go there anymore. It may be all right for Tommy, but it's about time you started acting like a girl instead of a roughneck."

"It isn't fair," Terry said furiously. "You let Tommy do anything he wants just because he's a boy. Well, all right then, I won't *be* a girl anymore. I'll cut my hair off and I'll — I'll run away and join the army," she finished, wildly flailing her arms.

Terry's mother, her voice going higher with each word, was saying, "Now, Teresa Seth, you calm DOWN!" when Tommy rushed in.

"Hey, Terry, I got you a paper route," he shouted breathlessly.

"Oh boy, oh boy, oh boy!" Terry yelled.

"It's just for a week," Tommy went on excitedly, "but it should give you a little money toward a bicy — "

He stopped when his mother collapsed on the sofa saying, "That's the last straw!"

"What's wrong with a bicycle?" Tommy asked, looking from his mother to Terry.

"It isn't the bicycle," Terry said grimly. "She's going to make me promise not to go down to the river anymore. And I bet you anything she's going to say I can't have the paper route. And IT ISN'T FAIR!"

Before their mother could say anything, Tommy said, "But, gee, Mom, if you make her promise not to go down to the river, that's like punishing her for saving Soupy's life. Why, she almost *died*."

"She *what*? Maybe you'd better tell me what happened, Tommy. Maybe I can get some sense out of you," his mother said.

So Tommy told all about it. Terry was amazed. He made her seem like a real heroine. She listened fascinated. Every little while her mother whispered, "Good heavens."

"So then," Tommy finished, "just as she was slipping off, we got to her and pulled her up. For a minute I thought we wouldn't be able to. She didn't have any strength left and couldn't help, and Soupy kept getting in the way. And there she was, all bloody and looking like she was going to faint or something."

"Good heavens," Mrs. Seth said weakly.

"And it wasn't her fault we went on the bridge. She just came after, real slow and careful. She's always much more careful than the rest of us," Tommy pointed out.

"Well, it's no wonder you're all worked up, Terry. I think you'd better go right to bed. First let's take a look at your scars." As Terry opened her mouth to object, her mother added, "I'm not sending you to bed to punish you, but you've had too much excitement. You can read, and I'll give you your supper in bed."

"Anyhow, you'll get out of drying the dishes," Tommy whispered. "And I bet she forgets all about making you promise about the river."

Mrs. Seth didn't say anything definite about whether they could or couldn't play by the river, but she gave them a hint of what would happen if they did something like climbing on a bridge again.

Just before she fell asleep, Terry remembered that her mother hadn't said if she could have the paper route. She wanted to ask her, but she was so tired. . . .

Paper Girl

"TERRY, WAKE UP! Don't you know what day it is?"

Terry sat up, bewildered, and stared at her mother. Then she remembered. This was a glorious day. In the afternoon she would start her paper route. This morning Tommy was taking her on his route to make sure she knew what to do.

She jumped out of bed and yawned noisily. Her cereal was on the table and she gulped it down.

"Chew thirty times," her mother said automatically, but not as though she had her mind on what she was saying.

"Hurry up, Terry," her brother said impatiently. He was already dressed and ready to go.

Terry tumbled into her clothes and struggled while her mother braided her hair.

"Ouch," Terry grumbled. "Do you have to pull?"

"You're the one who's pulling," her mother said. "Why can't you learn to braid it yourself? Honestly, the way you grab two hunks of hair and put the rubber bands around them — not even bothering to make a part first — "

Terry was ready to point out that when she did make a part, her mother complained it wasn't straight. So what was the use?

But she'd better not start anything this morning. Terry had obtained her mother's permission, but she felt that her paper route hung by a thread and she had been on her best behavior.

At last she and Tommy were on their way. They raced up the street in the cool, silent morning, with Tommy's news bag flapping against his leg as he ran.

They arrived in front of the drug store while Mr. Spring was still throwing stacks of papers off the truck. He delivered the papers to all the paper boys of the neighborhood here.

George, whose route Terry was going to have while he was at camp, was already there, with several other boys.

"Hey, Mr. Spring," George said, "this here's the girl's going to take my route."

Mr. Spring threw the last stack on the sidewalk and gave Terry a long, sober look.

"Well, you're mighty young," he said, "but I guess if you're Tommy's sister, you'll do. Otherwise I never would have agreed to a girl doing it." Then, still without smiling, he climbed in the truck and drove off.

"Boy, are you in good with him," George said to Tommy. "He sure never said anything that nice to me."

The other boys laughed, and one of them said, "You can't complain, George. I thought he was going to take your route away the time you threw that paper through an open window and broke somebody's lamp."

All the boys eyed Terry curiously. She knew some of them from school, but they were all at least two years ahead of her. She stared intently at the sidewalk while Tommy cut the wire around his papers.

"Aren't you going to help roll them?" he had to ask her. She had helped him roll papers before and they soon finished half of them. The rest they saved to roll on the way.

"Can I carry the bag?" Terry begged.

Tommy already had the bag over his shoulder. He looked at her dubiously and then took it off. "It's pretty heavy," he said. "But I guess you'll have to get used to it anyhow."

Terry confidently put the bag on her shoulder. Immediately her knees bent until the bag sagged to the ground. She blushed as the boys laughed at her. Then she straightened up and wobbled off down the street.

"C'mon," she called back to Tommy. "What are we waiting for?"

"Never mind," Tommy said, grinning himself, as he

caught up to her. "I did the same thing the first day, and I bet they all did too. It doesn't look as if it could possibly be that heavy, does it? You get used to it after a while."

Terry found that by shifting the bag from one shoulder to the other every little while, it wasn't too bad. She looked proudly down at the bag, remembering the day Tommy got it. She had helped him roll it in the dirt so it wouldn't look too new. By this afternoon she would have George's bag and his list of customers.

It was strange walking down the nearly deserted streets. It made it seem as though the world, or at least this part of it, belonged to her and Tommy. She told him the way she felt. It didn't seem silly talking about something like that in the unusual quiet.

"I often feel that way in the mornings," Tommy said. "Afternoons it's different. Sometimes in the mornings I pretend the houses aren't there and I'm the first person to walk this ground."

"That could be a buffalo," Terry said, as a big bus rumbled by.

They played the game until they reached the start of Tommy's route. He was very serious about his job and wasn't going to allow anything to take his mind off of it.

Terry watched as he carefully checked each address on his list, even though he already knew it by heart. He had had a hard time getting a route because he had been a year younger than the youngest of the other boys. But he had persistently hung around the drug store afternoons when the papers were delivered. Finally Mr. Spring let him deliver papers when one of the other boys was sick.

When a boy announced one day that he was moving and had to give up his route, Tommy was there. He didn't say a word. He told Terry afterward that he just stood there *willing* Mr. Spring to give him the route. At last Mr. Spring said grumpily that if Tommy wanted to try it, he would ask the supervisor at the paper if it was all right.

The supervisor said Tommy could have the route on trial. When Tommy found out he had to post a bond first, he went home as pale as a ghost. Terry and her mother were frantic, but there was nothing they could do, and Tommy knew it. And then Greg's father heard about it and paid for the bond without giving them a chance to refuse.

That was four months ago. Tommy was no longer on trial, and he had paid back Greg's father. He was so careful that he hadn't had a single complaint from his customers. If he kept his perfect record for two months more, the newspaper would give him a twenty-five-dollar savings bond. That was a lot of money, but Terry knew her brother didn't care as much about the prize as he did about proving he could handle the route.

Suddenly Tommy handed the list to her. "O.K., what's the next house?" he demanded.

Terry took her bearings from the nearest house. She

looked back at the list and quickly told him the next customer's address.

Tommy handed her a rolled-up paper and told her to throw it on the porch. Terry knew this would be the hardest part for her. Her brother threw the papers with ease, and they landed exactly where he intended them to. She drew back her arm the way he did and let the paper fly. It hit the edge of the porch, teetered a moment, and fell off behind a bush. She ran and crawled behind the bush, and put the paper by the door.

Then she ran back to Tommy and checked the list for the next address. The address meant nothing to her, but when she looked at the house, she realized it was where Miss Marshall, her next year's teacher,

lived. She hoped that Tommy would throw this paper, but he handed it to her.

"Why can't you throw it as well as when we're playing catch?" he asked. "Throw underhand, the way you always do. Pretend I'm standing on that porch, waiting for the ball — right there by the front door."

Terry took a pitching stance, kept her eye on the door, and let the paper fly. It sailed straight for the door. Terry gave a glad shout just as Miss Marshall opened the door.

Plop! The paper struck the teacher in the stomach and fell to the porch. Miss Marshall bent down and for a horrible moment Terry thought she'd been hurt. But she was only picking up the paper. She looked at Terry and Tommy standing there with their mouths open.

"Hello, Tom," she said mildly. "And you're his sister Teresa, aren't you?"

"Yes, Miss Marshall, and it was me that threw the paper and I'm awfully sorry but I didn't know you were coming out just then or I wouldn't uv," Terry said in a rush.

"It was *I* who threw the paper," Miss Marshall corrected.

"Uh, yeah, it was you, I mean — " Terry stopped because Miss Marshall was leaning against the door jamb, *laughing*.

"That's all right, Teresa, it was a good throw," Miss Marshall said when she could talk. "It will be a pleasure to have you in my class."

"Thank you," Terry answered, reddening. Why wouldn't her tongue do what it was told?

Miss Marshall went back inside, saving Terry from further embarrassment. Tommy still hadn't said a word.

"I couldn't help it," Terry said.

"I know it," Tommy replied. "I was just thinking it could have happened to me any time and I never even thought about it. Gosh!"

Terry threw the papers as gently as possible after that. She had to pick up some of them, but Tommy didn't give her any more suggestions. Soon they were at their building, which was part of Tommy's route. Here the papers were delivered flat instead of being rolled up.

"That wasn't so bad," Terry said as they finished. "Except for Miss Marshall."

"No, it isn't so hard," Tommy said. "You just have to be careful, that's all."

Tommy went out to see where the gang was. Terry stayed in to figure once more how much money she would make. Tommy had made her figure it out herself to give her practice on her arithmetic, so she still didn't trust the figures.

Taking a clean sheet of paper, Terry started all over again. In the morning she had thirty-seven customers, in the evening fifty-four. And on Sunday, fifty-nine. She came out with the same amount. At a penny for each weekday paper and four cents for the Sunday papers, she should have $7.82 for her week's work.

Tommy had said that wouldn't buy a bike, even second hand, but it was a good start.

Just then Tommy came in, tossed her a paper bag and a notebook, and said, "George brought 'em down. We're over climbing trees," and he dashed out again.

Terry put the bag on her shoulder and looked at herself in the mirror on the door to the hall. It didn't look bad at all. It would have looked better if the bag weren't almost down to her ankles. She stood there, looking in the mirror and turning over the pages of house numbers in the notebook. What if she did such a good job delivering papers that Mr. Spring would say, "Well, we could certainly use someone like you to take over a regular route?"

But she didn't think he would say that, no matter how good a job she did. And all because she was a girl. If he did say it, her mother wouldn't let her take a route anyway.

Suddenly, still looking at herself in the mirror, she thought of something nice she could do for her mother.

Her mother complained about having to braid Terry's hair, and Terry didn't think she would ever learn to do it herself. Whenever she tried it, there was always a lot of hair left over. And one braid would be pointing forward and one backward so that it looked ridiculous and had to be undone anyway.

She found a pair of scissors and cut the braids short,

letting them unwind. There, that would save her mother a lot of worry.

Then she sat down to read a book, pausing only to make a peanut butter sandwich for lunch. Finally Tommy came in and told her it was time to go and collect their papers.

Tommy took a good look at her and asked, "What happened to you?" She had almost forgotten the haircut by this time. Tommy wasn't sure it was such a good idea. "What did you cut it with, a hacksaw?" he asked.

Terry tried to see the back of her head in the mirror. But as soon as she turned her head far enough, she couldn't see herself. She tried turning her head quickly, but it still didn't work.

"We haven't got time now," Tommy said, "but I'll straighten it up a little when we get home."

Outside, Soupy was stirring an ant hill with his finger. As the ants scurried away, he made some crawl on his hands and shook them off over the ruins of their home.

"Build it up again," he ordered them. "I want to watch."

"Soupy, don't do that," Terry said. "Those poor ants have a hard enough time without you making it worse."

"Can I come with?" Soupy howled. "Can I? Can I? I'll help you. I know how to do it."

"You don't know how," Terry said. "But you can come with me if you promise to be good. Go in and ask your father and then catch up to us."

Soupy tore inside and they hadn't gone very far before he ran up to them.

They reached the drug store just after Mr. Spring had left. Tommy cut the wire around Terry's papers and his own and they started rolling some of them. Soupy wasn't allowed to help because he was so clumsy, and he was dancing with impatience to be off.

"I'm a paper boy," he announced to anyone within shouting distance.

"Oh, you are not," Terry said. "You're a paper girl's helper."

Soupy was just as happy with this title. "I'm a paper girl's HELPER!" he screamed.

Terry covered her ears and closed her eyes to shut out all the laughing faces. "Shut up, Soupy!" she bellowed.

As soon as she could, she hurried off with her papers, dragging Soupy after her. "Now be good," she told him. "Do what you're told and *nothing* else."

Soupy trotted silently at her side up the few blocks to where her route started. Her customers were in the direction away from the apartment, three blocks up and down a hill, then over a block, and up and down the hill again, and back one block to where she had started. She had been in this neighborhood before only on her way to the swimming pool.

Terry checked each address on her list carefully, threw the paper, and continued on to the next house. "Slowly and carefully," Tommy had said, and that is what she did. Whenever a paper missed the porch, she told Soupy to go and pick it up, while she went on to the next house.

Keeping her eyes glued to her list and the house numbers, she almost stumbled a few times over cracks in the sidewalk. The only time she looked up was when she reached a curb and jarred the top of her head by unexpectedly stepping down.

At last she was back where she started and through for the day. "See, when you know how to do it, there's nothing to it," she boasted to Soupy.

Her smile froze and she stared at him in alarm.

"Soupy, what are you doing with those papers?" she demanded. He was holding nine or ten papers in his arms.

"You told me to pick them up," Soupy said brightly.

"How can you be so stupid?" she wailed. "You were suppose to put them on the porches, not take them with you. What do you think I was *delivering* them for?" She was so angry that she began shaking him.

Soupy collapsed in a sobbing heap on the sidewalk, his face buried in the newspapers. "I couldn't help it," he said jerkily. "You told me to pick them up. I'm sorry, Terry."

Ashamed for having yelled at him when he was too little to know any better, Terry knelt down beside him and wiped his tears with the hem of her shirt.

"It's O.K., Soupy," she said. "We'll put them back where they belong. Goodness, I hope we can figure out where they go."

Putting the newspapers in the bag, Terry and Soupy started on the route for the second time. There was no joy in it this time, only determination and a feeling of panic for Terry, as she wondered if this would somehow spoil her brother's perfect record. At least she didn't have to worry about George's record. He had an awful one.

Most of the people had already taken their papers in. Terry went up to house after house on her list, asking if they had received their paper. The people were nice about it, but they asked her so many questions about why she was delivering papers that the job was taking forever.

When it was over, there was one paper left. She knew she had been very careful, going up to every house where there was no paper. When no one had come to the door she had left a paper there, and given papers to all the people who said they hadn't received one. Tommy frequently had a paper left over, and she was sure it was all right, but she would have been happier if they had come out even.

"Well, we'd better hurry home, Soupy," she said. "I don't know what your father will say about bringing you back so late."

They ran part of the way and walked fast when they were winded. Terry brought Soupy to his apartment without stopping off at her own.

"I'm awfully sorry, but — " Terry began apologizing to Soupy's father.

"That's all right, Terry," he said, even though he had looked rather anxious when he came to the door. "I knew Kevin was in good hands. But you had better hurry home. Your mother was here a short while ago. She was worried about you."

Terry flew down the hall and rushed in, ready to tell what had happened and get a little sympathy.

"It's about time," her mother said. "Where on earth have you been all this while?"

"I suppose you loused it all up as usual," her brother growled at the same time.

"What happened to your hair?" her mother yelled.

Terry threw her paper bag on the floor and burst into tears. "I wish I hadn't even come home," she sobbed. "I wish a truck had run over me and then you'd be sorry. I'm going to run away. That ought to make you happy, both of you, always yelling at me." She turned and started out the door again.

"You come back here and wash your hands and sit down at the table. While I'm heating up your supper again, you can do some explaining," her mother ordered.

Terry turned back slowly. She wasn't sure she wanted to run away when it was going to be dark so soon. Anyway, it wouldn't hurt to eat first. She washed her hands and sat down. Her mother poured some milk for her and told her to calm down before she started talking. Tommy sat at the table and glowered at her.

"If you're through eating," his mother said to him, "go in the other room. Just because you made a mistake is no reason to get mad at her."

Tommy left, muttering as he did so, "I didn't make a mistake. I *know* I left her a paper."

"Oh, no," Terry cried, forgetting she was angry at everyone, "you didn't get a complaint!"

Tommy came back and sat down across from her. "I always check, don't I? I check and double-check. You know, you've seen me. But Mr. Spring just called, said he was leaving the office when he heard there was a complaint on my route. He asked about it and found out it was that Mrs. Pinehurst downstairs, that new lady who just started taking last week. She saw the other papers in the hall and there wasn't any by her door, so right away she called up. But I *must* have left her one."

"Everybody makes mistakes," his mother said. "Why should you be any different? Mr. Spring said the same thing, didn't he? He told you not to worry too much since it's the first mistake you've made. It is a shame you won't get the bond, but it was an awful lot to expect when you're new at it."

"But he does check, Mom," Terry protested. "And why didn't she just come and tell him, instead of calling the paper. Then it wouldn't have gone on his record."

"Remember, she's new here," Mrs. Seth said, putting Terry's supper on the table. "She probably doesn't know who Tommy is, or anything about the records. All she knew was she didn't get her paper. And let's not get off the subject. I want to know why you're so late."

As she ate, Terry explained first what had happened on her route. "That won't hurt your record, will it?" she asked her brother.

"No," Tommy said. "I don't think there'd be any complaints about that. Anyhow, they'd go on George's record, not mine. It's his route. But it was a pretty dumb idea to bring Soupy along."

"I guess I should have watched him," Terry admitted. "But I didn't think about anything except the list and the houses. Oh, and I got a paper left over, 'case you want to give it to Mrs. Pinehurst."

"Good idea," Tommy said. "I was going to go out and get one."

While Tommy went downstairs, Terry tried to explain to her mother about the haircut. Somehow, as she told it, it didn't sound like such a favor for her mother. More like something to save herself time and work.

"But I couldn't make pigtails," she finished. "I just couldn't."

Her mother sighed. "You had such pretty hair," she said. "Especially when it was curled for Sunday. Scolding you won't bring it back. But did you ever try *hard* to braid it? You can work hard when it's something you want, but otherwise you just don't seem to bother."

Terry stared at her empty plate and didn't say anything. She felt her mother was right.

"Well, next time you get such a crazy idea, ask me first. Try thinking before you do something, instead of rushing into it," her mother said wearily.

Later, while her mother was trimming her hair with the scissors, Terry promised herself that she would think before she acted after this. If only she could remember to think about thinking in time.

Watson and Sherlock

"**I** KNOW I left her a paper. I finished off upstairs and went down again, and it was gone. And that makes the third time now," Tommy said, indignantly, the following Friday.

"Well, then, somebody must be taking them," Terry said.

"Guess I'll have to save her paper until she comes home every day," Tommy said. "Then I won't have to keep going out to get her another one."

The more Terry thought about that, the more she didn't like it. It was like giving up without even trying. And what was to stop whoever was taking the papers from taking somebody else's instead?

"Why don't we catch the thief?" she said excitedly. "We can keep watch and — "

"How can I keep watch if the paper's gone before I get through delivering?" Tommy interrupted.

"For Pete's sake, I can watch alone until you get back," Terry said. "By Monday I'll be finished with my own route." Honestly, sometimes he acted as if she was a moron or something.

"Well, O.K. It's just for a few minutes," Tommy said reluctantly.

They decided there was no need to watch mornings because the papers always disappeared in the afternoon. On Saturday and Sunday Mrs. Pinehurst was home, and Tommy knocked on her door as he left her paper.

So on Monday afternoon when Tommy left a paper by Mrs. Pinehurst's door, Terry was sitting on the steps going up from the first floor where she could keep an eye on the entire length of the hall. Tommy joined her a few minutes later.

Terry was glad to see him. She had realized in the short while she was alone that they hadn't planned what to do when they did catch the thief.

"I'll just tell him to stop," Tommy said when she asked him about it. "But don't you do it. If you see somebody take the paper when I'm not here, you wait for me and tell me who it was."

Terry was willing to agree to this. They watched in silence for a while. There was little activity in the building at this hour before people began arriving home from work.

Danny came tiptoeing up the stairs. "Anything doing?" he whispered. Tommy shook his head.

"Sure you don't want any help?" Danny said, still in whispers.

"No," Tommy whispered back. "It would be too noisy with the whole gang here. We'd never catch him."

Danny looked disappointed, but he turned and tiptoed downstairs.

Another silence. A man came out of his apartment. He went out the back way without passing Mrs. Pinehurst's door, which was only a few doors down from the front stairs.

Another man came out and passed Mrs. Pinehurst's door without hesitating. He smiled at them on his way out.

Terry said, thinking aloud, "We only have to worry about people who don't take the paper from you. If they did, they wouldn't have to steal it."

"You'd make a good detective," Tommy said. "Tell you what, you be Watson and I'll be Sherlock."

"Who — what?" Terry said.

"You know, Sherlock Holmes and Dr. Watson," Tommy explained. When Terry still looked blank, he said, "Don't you even read Sherlock Holmes? You should, he's a darn good detective. Dr. Watson was this dumb friend of his — well, you don't have to be just like him," Tommy added hastily.

Tommy told her about some of the cases Sherlock

Holmes had solved. Then they tried to apply his methods to their own case.

"The papers disappear at all different times," Terry said, "but before most of the working people come home. So it has to be somebody who doesn't work."

"Or somebody who works funny hours. Trouble is, the way people move in and out, we don't know hardly anything about most of them. I don't think we can figure it out this way. We'll just have to watch and try to catch him," Tommy said.

At this point Mrs. Pinehurst went by and it was time for Terry and Tommy to go upstairs for dinner.

While they ate, their mother asked why they had been sitting on the stairs, and they told her.

"I don't blame you for trying to find out who's taking the papers," she said. "But I don't want either of you doing anything about it. If you find out who it is, let me know and I'll take care of it."

"Oh, for Pete's sake, Mom — " Tommy began.

"You heard me," his mother said. "Furthermore, if you were taking papers, would you do it while somebody was sitting there watching? I wouldn't."

Tommy and Terry looked at each other sheepishly. Of course the thief wasn't going to do anything with them in plain sight. What on earth had they been thinking of?

As Mrs. Seth put some more mashed potatoes on their plates, she said, "Tommy, why won't you let me go talk to Mrs. Pinehurst? I'm sure if she knew her papers were stolen and it wasn't your fault at all, she'd be glad to call the paper and explain to them."

"Sure, or I could think of some reason to go talk to her and just happen to mention it," Terry said.

"You stay outta my route," Tommy told his sister. And to his mother, "It's too late to do anything. She already complained. If a customer wants to make a complaint, that's up to the customer."

"Well, I think you're wrong," his mother said, but she left it there. She had her own plans.

The next afternoon Terry and Tommy stationed themselves a few steps up from the landing, where the stairs turned. They each brought a book to while away the time and took turns peeking.

Soon they were engrossed in their reading and had lost track of whose turn it was to peek. When they remembered to look, the paper was gone.

"This sure isn't going to work," Tommy said.

He sounded so discouraged that Terry tried to think of something to cheer him up. The best she could do was, "Maybe tomorrow, if we don't bring anything to read — "

"But it happens so fast," Tommy said. "No, I've got a better idea. Let's set a trap."

"What kind of a trap?" Terry asked.

"I don't know," Tommy said. "But I'm going to run up to the library and get Sherlock Holmes out again, to see if I can get some ideas from him."

While he was gone, Terry thought about the problem. When Tommy came back to their apartment with Sherlock Holmes and a book on the F.B.I., Terry greeted him with, "What about flour?"

"Well, what about flour?" Tommy said, leafing through Sherlock.

"We could put some flour in the paper and it would leave a trail leading right to the thief," Terry said. As Tommy gave her a disgusted look, she said, "What's wrong with that?"

"Nothing," Tommy said. Why did she have to go figure it out before he even had a chance to do any research? But he had to admit it was a good idea.

They decided to try it out the next afternoon. Terry couldn't wait until Tommy returned from his route, so she went up to the drug store with him.

Terry started rolling papers while Tommy looked at the classified ads. He had enough money saved to buy an inexpensive new bike, but he was hoping to save some money by buying a used one.

"Oh no! I *would* have to find one today," Tommy exclaimed. "It's more than I wanted to pay, but it sure sounds good. A European racer, look." He showed Terry the ad.

"Sounds perfect," Terry said. "You going to go look at it?"

"How can I? It's way on the other side of town. By the time I finish delivering papers, set the trap, and catch the thief, eat supper, and take a bus out there, somebody else will have bought it. Anyway, the bank will be closing now and I wouldn't be able to have the money for the bike."

"I don't know why everybody calls you a brain when you can't even *think*," Terry said furiously, crushing the paper she was rolling. "I'll deliver the papers, and if you're home late, I'll tell Mom where you are."

"Yes, but — " Tommy said.

"Hurry up and get to the bank before it closes," Terry snapped.

Tommy ran down the street toward the bank. He called back, "You better not set you-know-what to-day. Tomorrow we'll do it."

Terry smiled and waved. He could take that for a yes if he wanted to. She picked up the paper bag and started out.

Tommy made her so angry sometimes, she thought. He had agreed readily enough to her delivering his papers. But why hadn't he thought of it himself? If he thought she couldn't set the trap by herself, he could just think again. She was going to do it. Anyhow, if it didn't work, nobody had to know about it.

"Oh, klunk!" Terry said aloud. She'd been thinking so hard, she'd walked past the start of the route. Not only that, she'd rolled up every last paper and now she'd have to unroll the ones for the apartment. Her mother was always telling her to think, but how could you think and do anything at the same time?

Terry went back and started delivering the papers. When she came to Miss Marshall's house, she didn't try to throw the paper. She walked up to the porch, set the paper down gently, and walked away.

She finished the route without mishap and took Mrs. Pinehurst's paper to her apartment. There she put plenty of flour between the pages and swept up the flour she had spilled. But as soon as she picked up the paper more flour drifted down to the floor.

"This sure was a good idea," Terry thought, "but how am I going to get the paper downstairs?" Finally she took the paper down in a shopping bag and went to her place behind the landing.

The tenth time Terry peeked out, old Mrs. Larpenteur was standing over Mrs. Pinehurst's paper. Mrs. Larpenteur went to Terry's church, and at the end of Mass when everybody else was muttering "amen" after the prayers, Mrs. Larpenteur always shouted out, "You said it." It made everybody jump each time even though they knew it was coming. But Mrs. Larpenteur was so old and so deaf that nobody liked to say anything about it to her. It would be awful, Terry thought, if Mrs. Larpenteur turned out to be the paper thief.

Mrs. Larpenteur jockeyed the paper around with her foot and bent over. Then she straightened up and walked away. Terry breathed a sigh of relief. Mrs. Larpenteur was just reading the paper.

A little later when Terry peeked out, there was a man walking down the hall. Was he slowing down by Mrs. Pinehurst's door? No, he walked on.

Terry leaned back. She hoped something would happen soon. After counting to fifty slowly, she looked out again.

The paper was gone.

On the hall carpeting was a trail of flour, leading from Mrs. Pinehurst's door down the stairs. Terry tore outside.

It was hard to find traces of flour on the sidewalk. The only person in sight was a man walking towards the corner. At least Terry could see if he was carrying a paper. As she raced after him, she saw her mother and Mrs. Pinehurst get off a bus at the corner.

Not only was the man carrying a paper, but here was absolute proof. Terry saw that her mother and Mrs. Pinehurst were practically up to them. Dancing in front of the man, she called out, "Mister, hey, mister, you got flour all over your suit!"

Mrs. Seth and Mrs. Pinehurst both stopped. "Terry, really!" her mother said.

Before her mother could say any more, Terry said, "Isn't it funny, I put flour in Mrs. Pinehurst's paper and here this man has flour all over his suit."

Her mother caught on right away even though she hadn't known about the flour. "Now that is a strange thing," she said. "How could the flour from Mrs. Pinehurst's paper get on his suit?"

"Flour in my paper?" Mrs. Pinehurst said, bewildered.

"I don't know what you're talking about," the

man said stiffly. His face a burning red, he walked on, trying to look dignified while he brushed at his suit, rubbing the flour in.

Terry started after him, but her mother caught her by the shoulder. "Let well enough alone," Mrs. Seth said. "I don't think he'll be taking any more papers."

"What's going on?" Mrs. Pinehurst asked.

Terry explained that her papers had been stolen, and told her about the trap. Then Terry and her mother began talking at once about Tommy's perfect record and the bond and the complaint. Finally Mrs. Seth let Terry tell it.

"I think that's terrible," Mrs. Pinehurst said. "I'll call the paper first thing and see if I can get it straightened out. But why didn't somebody tell me?"

"Tommy wouldn't let us talk to you about it and he wouldn't do it himself," Mrs. Seth said. "He worked so hard for his perfect record and when something went wrong, I guess he just gave up. I thought perhaps I could run into you accidentally and tell you. I must have been down in the basement washroom twenty times this week, hoping you'd be there washing clothes. And then when we got off the bus together just now, I was about to tell you when I saw how oddly Terry was behaving."

They had reached the apartment building and they all went in.

"Terry," Mrs. Seth said, looking at the steps, "how much flour did you put in the paper?"

"I had to put enough to leave a trail," Terry said.

"We'd better clean it up," her mother said. "You go upstairs and get the broom."

"I'll get mine too," Mrs. Pinehurst said. "It won't take us long."

While Mrs. Seth and Mrs. Pinehurst swept, Terry held the dustpan and the shopping bag they were using to put the flour in, since it had flour in it already.

"I can't understand why he wanted to steal the papers," Mrs. Pinehurst said. "He lives next door to me. He's a salesman. I'm sure he makes a lot more money than I do. At least he can afford a hi-fi set. He drives me crazy with it, playing it so loud late at night."

"Well, you never know about people," Mrs. Seth said.

"I'm sorry so much flour got spilled," Terry said, after they had finished cleaning up and gone home.

"It doesn't matter," her mother replied. "I'm just glad that business is all straightened out. But where is Tommy? Why wasn't he with you?"

Just then there was an insistent beep-beep-beep of a horn from outside and Tommy's voice calling, "Mom! Terry! Come see what I've got."

Terry ran to the window and saw Tommy out front with a bike. She and her mother went outdoors.

"What kind of bicycle is that?" Mrs. Seth said. "I never saw one like it." The bike had no fenders and the handlebars turned down and were taped.

"It's a racing bike. You can make it go ten different speeds with this gear shift. And it's got a horn and a pump, and this in back of the seat is a tool case," Tommy said.

"Boy, it sure is a beauty," Terry said.

"It certainly is a big day for you, Tommy," his mother said. "First Terry found out who's been taking your papers, and now this."

Tommy looked daggers at his sister. "You mean you went ahead and set the trap after I told you not to?" he asked.

"You thought I couldn't do it by myself, and I did, so there!" Terry retorted.

"Who said anything about you couldn't do it?" Tommy said heatedly. "The flour was your idea in the first place. I just wanted to be there to see it, too, you big stupe."

"Oh," Terry said, taken aback. She hadn't proved anything to him. Instead she'd been awfully mean. Trying to make amends, she said, "Did you ride the bike all the way home?"

"How else would I get it here?" he said sarcastically. "My back aches from it though. You have to ride it way bent over. But I'll get used to it."

Terry ran her hands along the tape on the handlebars. Tommy had a bike now. All the boys had bikes. Even Cindy and Kim had bikes. Suddenly she realized that the whole world had bikes except Terry Seth. She burst into tears and ran into the building.

Tommy's anger vanished. "Hey, you can ride it, Terry," he yelled. "You want to ride it right now?"

Terry kept on running. She slammed into her apartment and threw herself down on the sofa and sobbed. She had cried until she was exhausted. Then she went into the other room to dry her face with a towel.

Tommy was sitting on his bed, frowning intently at a book. The book was upside down. His mother, her face set, was at the stove pounding mashed potatoes as though she wanted to pound the bottom out of the pan. She looked angrier than Terry could remember.

"What'd I do now?" Terry asked. "You're always getting mad at me about something. What'd I *do?*"

Her mother went on pounding. "I'm not mad at you," she said. "I'm not mad at anyone." She turned and said fiercely, "Do you think I don't want you to have a bicycle? Do you think I wouldn't go out right now and buy you one if I could?"

"Oh," Terry said. "Well, it — it doesn't matter. It's just — "

"Don't be silly, of course it matters," her mother said. "Every child wants a bicycle. I wanted one when I was little."

"Did you get one?" Tommy asked, putting down his book.

"No," Mrs. Seth said. "None of us had bicycles. I was lucky to have a doll. One of the neighbor girls gave me hers when she outgrew it." Terry's mother tried to smile. "You could set the table," she suggested.

Setting the table had been one of Terry's jobs, but

74

her mother had said it was easier to do it herself than to keep after Terry to do it.

Terry got out the plates and silver. She was sorry to see her mother so upset, but it was nice to have her understand how she felt about the bike. "Terry," her mother broke in, "what do you think Tommy is going to do with two forks and the butcher knife?"

Terry looked at what she had done. The whole table was set crazily. "That's just in case the frank-furters are tough," she said.

Her mother laughed. "I don't think you'll find the potatoes lumpy," she said.

Over their meal they talked about anything but bicycles. After they finished and while Terry was dry-ing the dishes, Tommy said to her, "If we can go, I'll take you down to the popcorn truck on my bike and get us some popcorn."

The rule was that they had to stay in front of the building after supper. But their mother said, "I guess it would be all right for once, if you come right back."

Terry helped her brother take the bike up the base-ment steps. Tommy got on and Terry climbed up and sat sidesaddle on the bar in front of him.

Tommy tried to lean over to get both hands on the Handle bars. Terry was in the way.

"I'll steer," Terry said. "You just pedal."

"We can try it at least," Tommy agreed. He held on to her shoulders while she steered.

It wasn't easy to steer a bike riding sidesaddle. The

bike wobbled and Terry wobbled with it. Tommy, having nothing to hold on to but wobbly shoulders on a wobbly bike, pedaled hard while he jerked back and forth trying to keep his balance.

They reached a corner. The bike made a sharp turn one way. Terry and Tommy went the other.

"My bike!" Tommy groaned. He and Terry scram-scrambled to their feet.

"I could be killed dead and all you worry about is your bike," Terry complained.

"How could you be hurt?" Tommy asked while he looked over his bike, inch by inch. "You fell on me."

Fortunately the bike was all right. "I guess it's just a one-rider bike," Tommy said. "You ride it slow down to the river and I'll walk. My back still aches from riding it this afternoon anyway."

Terry had no choice but to ride slowly. Her legs weren't long enough, and as each pedal came up she had to catch her foot under it and pull it up to the top, then push down hard on it while trying to catch her foot under the other pedal.

"I'm sorry," Tommy said. "I never thought it would be too big for you."

"Maybe my legs will stretch this way," Terry said.

When they came to the river, Greg was there, talking to Mr. Yonson, the popcorn man. Greg was chewing on popcorn and talking at the same time. "Everybody'll have to wear costumes to my party," he said. "On account of it's a costume party."

"What party? When's it going to be?" Tommy asked.

76

Greg turned, smiling. Then he saw Terry and looked away quickly. "Well, I gotta be going," he said. He got on his bike and rode off.

"Can you beat that!" Tommy said. "I wonder if he's having a party and not inviting the gang."

"Who else could he invite?" Terry said. "Besides, he didn't act funny till he saw me."

"Yeah, and that wasn't very nice of him," Tommy said. "You can't help the face you got."

"Now, now," Mr. Yonson said before Terry could reply. "Who wants a handful of popcorn?"

"Oh, we came to buy some," Tommy told him. He handed over the money and Mr. Yonson gave him a box of hot popcorn.

"Will you sing us your song? Please," Terry begged.

"Well," Mr. Yonson said. He always sang his song when requested, after a good deal of teasing reluctance. But now he looked at Terry, her eyes still red from crying. "Tell you what," he said. "I'll sing for you if you do something for me. It's time for me to go home and I can't go until my truck is cranked. So if you'll do that for me, young lady, I'll sing for you."

Mr. Yonson handed her the crank and Tommy helped her find the place in front of the truck to put it.

"This must be a pretty old truck, Mr. Yonson," Tommy said.

"When I was young, the truck was young with me," Mr. Yonson said.

"Golly, and it still works!" Terry said.

"And why shouldn't it? *I* do," Mr. Yonson said,

scowling. "You just start cranking now, and I'll sing."

Terry and Tommy cranked and Mr. Yonson took a deep breath and sang:

> My name is Yon Yonson,
> I live in Visconsin,
> I vork in the lumber mills there.
> As I valk down the street,
> All the people I meet,
> They are asking my name and I'm saying —
> My name is Yon Yonson,
> I live in Visconsin —

Cough, shudder, sputter went the truck. Terry handed the crank to Mr. Yonson and he drove down the street singing.

> I vork in the lumber mills there.
> As I valk down the street,
> All the people I meet,
> They are asking my name and I'm saying —

"That was fun, wasn't it," Terry said on the way home as they pushed the bike between them and ate their popcorn.

"Yes it was," Tommy said. "But I'm still wondering what's up with Greg."

"Maybe he'll say something tomorrow," Terry said.

The street lights went on when they were a block away from home. They quickly put the bike away in the basement and went upstairs.

That night when Terry climbed into bed, her mother and brother were talking in the other room. She couldn't hear what they were saying so she decided to get a glass of water. Opening the door quietly, she heard Tommy say, "But if I get it, it will be because of her, so it's only fair — "

"You were going to use it to start your college fund and that's more important," his mother said. "We'll just have to find — " She saw Terry and didn't finish.

"I want a glass of water," Terry said.

"Go ahead," said Mrs. Seth.

Terry drank her water in silence and went back to bed. Now what's going on? she wondered. First Greg, and now her mother and Tommy. Was she going to go through life having people stop talking as soon as she came by?

The Boys' Party

BY THE NEXT AFTERNOON when Tommy had to leave to pick up his papers, Greg still hadn't said anything about a party. Terry and the boys went on climbing trees after Tommy left.

Terry looked at the others in the surrounding trees high above her and wished that she could climb as high in hers. Out of all the trees in the woods this was the only one on which she could reach the third branch. In the others the first branch was too high or the branches were too far apart. This one was known as Terry's tree because she always climbed on it.

"Hey, Terry, can you do this?" Mike called down.

Terry didn't bother to look up. Mike was always scaring her by hanging by his knees on a high limb and then pretending to lose his balance. "The other monkeys can do it better," she said.

"Yuk, yuk, yuk," Mike sneered. "Listen to the high-wire artist."

"So what? I never broke three arms in one summer," Terry retorted.

"Hey, Mike, you been holding out? Let's see that third arm," Danny said.

Suddenly Terry noticed how dark it was getting. "It's going to rain any minute," she said. Her words were drowned out in a roar of thunder.

"Head for the hills, boys, it's a hurricane!" Greg screamed, as the rain started pelting down. "Race you to my house." They slid and tumbled out of the trees.

Terry didn't know what to do. She never knew whether to go with them or not when Tommy wasn't there. Greg turned and called to her, "You coming?" She decided that was an invitation.

By the time they scrambled into Greg's house, they had forgotten it was a race. Greg's mother, Mrs. Zimmer, was in the living room pulling electric plugs out of their sockets.

She jumped as Greg crept up behind her and yelled, "Look out, Mom, the electricity's escaping!"

"Really, Greg," his mother said. "Hello, boys. Hello, Terry. How about some pop?"

"Swell," Greg said for all of them. "Boy, we sure don't wait for a storm to knock out our electricity. We do it ourselves. Hope nobody planned on watching television."

"Never mind, Greg," his mother said. "I don't like to take chances." She went out to get the pop.

Danny went over to look at a bookcase in the corner. Sliding the glass doors back and forth, he said, "I see your dad finally finished it." Mr. Zimmer had been working on the bookcase for years. At least, he had started it years ago, almost finished it, and then left it. Most of his spare time was spent making things in his garage and basement, and they were full of partly completed projects. He never minded if the gang watched him work and sometimes he let them help.

"Not exactly," Greg said. "Mom finished it. Was Dad ever mad. He said he was just about to start working on it again."

The room was dim and the windows were black except when the lightning flashed and crackled. They decided to play a game of add-on ghost story, each picking up the story where the last one left off.

They had been playing a while when Terry stopped at, "So he turned on his flashlight and saw — " Danny began, "A headless monster . . ." just as Mrs. Zimmer came in again.

"Terry, can I talk to you for a minute?" Mrs. Zimmer said.

Terry looked at the others, but they were as surprised as she. Slowly and awkwardly she got off the floor, stamped her feet to wake them up, and followed Mrs. Zimmer to the kitchen. She liked Greg's mother. Mrs. Zimmer and Mr. O'Halloran were the emergency people for Terry and Tommy when their mother was at work. They had a telephone at home just so they could call their mother if they had to, but that was for matters of life and death. Otherwise Mrs. Seth was not allowed to use the phone at work, and they had never had to call her there. Greg's mother and Soupy's father provided iodine, bandages, and so forth.

Mrs. Zimmer didn't seem to know how to begin. She looked at Terry and then at the electric clock which wasn't running now, and picked up a hot-pad, twisting it nervously.

Finally she said, "You know, Terry, it isn't anything to do with you. I mean, everyone likes you, but — Well, Mr. Zimmer never played with girls when he was little."

Mrs. Zimmer paused. Terry stared at her, fearing what might be coming.

Greg's mother went on, "Anyway, he's having a costume party for Greg on the Fourth of July. A boys' party. No girls. I thought I'd tell you before the others, so at least it won't be a surprise. I'm sorry, Terry."

"It's all right," Terry said. "It doesn't matter."

Even as she went back to the others, stumbling over a hassock in her shock, Terry realized it might have been worse. Mr. Zimmer might have decided that Greg shouldn't play with girls at all, and then what would have happened? She knew it was only because she was Tommy's sister that the boys put up with her tagging along.

Suddenly she realized they were all staring at her.

She looked at the window just for somewhere to look and saw that the storm was almost over.

"I'm going home," she said. "I'm in the middle of a chapter." She went out and walked slowly home, sloshing through every puddle she could find.

Maybe if she tried hard and learned to do things as well as the boys, Mr. Zimmer would change his mind. No, it wasn't any use. She'd never be any good at climbing trees, and she would never learn to catch a fly ball without dropping it as soon as the sting burned her hands.

Tommy was just leaving as she arrived home. "You know where I was during the worst part of the rain?" he asked. "Miss Marshall's. She made me come in. It was pretty awful at first, but then she started talking about history. Did you know there's a lot of stuff they don't put in our books?"

"That's good," Terry said shortly. "They put too much junk in 'em as it is."

"What's eating you?" her brother asked. "Know where the guys are?"

"Over at Greg's," she answered.

She didn't feel like reading or doing anything else. She looked out the window at the gloomy day and gloomed along with it.

When her mother came home, her first words were, "Look at your feet! How many times do I have to tell you? If you must walk through puddles, take off your shoes. Or better yet, act like a young lady and walk on dry land. You know I can't afford to buy you an extra pair of shoes for play, the way you wear them out so fast."

Terry sat down on the sofa, jerked off her shoes, threw them on the floor, and folded her arms and scowled.

"That's fine. Now you can clean them while I make supper," her mother said.

When Tommy came in, Terry was cleaning her shoes, still scowling.

"I heard about the party, Terry," her brother said. "Gosh, I'm sorry. I think it's a dumb idea, but you can't tell Greg's dad that." He told his mother about the boys' party.

"That's a shame, Terry," her mother said. "Of course you feel bad about it, but that doesn't mean you have to take it out on us."

Sorry, Terry thought. Everybody's sorry. What good does sorry do? To get away from them, she got out a book and buried her face in it.

"Anyway, it's just like I've tried to tell you. Boys should play with boys, and girls with girls. You should spend your time playing with Kim and Cindy. Maybe they could teach you a few things, like walking around puddles," Mrs. Seth said. Terry pretended she hadn't heard.

In the days before the party, Terry was able to get used to the idea. She didn't like it any better, but she couldn't stay grumpy forever. Tommy went out of his way to be nice to her, especially after the supervisor from the paper called and said they were clearing his record. When Tommy asked if she would help him fix up a costume, she agreed readily. Their mother said they could use anything they found in the ragbag, which was a shopping bag full of wornout clothes, blankets, towels, and things, from which Mrs. Seth tore off rags as she needed them.

They made a pirate vest by removing the sleeves and buttons from an old blouse of Terry's. A piece of black velvet and shoelaces made an eye patch.

"You'll have to have a sash," Terry said. "You can use the one on my yellow dress."

"O.K.," Tommy said. "I'll have to figure out something to use for a sword too."

"That's easy," Terry said. "Take the butcher knife."

"You crazy or something?" Tommy asked. "Mom'd have ten fits if I did that."

"If you asked her, she'd say you could. She never says no to you," Terry said.

"Listen, she wouldn't say no I can't use the butcher knife, because I'm not dumb enough to ask her," Tommy said. "I'll find some cardboard and make a sword out of that."

On the afternoon of the Fourth of July Mrs. Seth was ironing the pirate vest when Tommy and Terry returned from delivering papers. Danny had helped, too, and they finished in record time. Tommy set to work gluing aluminum foil on his cardboard sword. Terry couldn't bear to watch.

"Why don't you go play with Cindy and Kim today?" her mother suggested.

"I don't even know if they're home," Terry said. She wished she could play with them. Soupy was at his grandmother's on a long visit, and Tommy wouldn't be home until late. He was going to eat at Greg's and afterwards they would burn sparklers. But Cindy and Kim were probably mad at her by now. She had run into them a few times since school let out. When they asked her to play she had said she was too busy.

She picked up her copy of *Little Women*. It gave her a guilty feeling every time she saw it. Before Cindy's last birthday Terry's mother had bought two books. Terry could choose the one she wanted and give Cindy the other. Afterward Terry admitted to herself that she knew all along Cindy already had a

copy of the ballet book. When Cindy opened her present, she had at first looked cold and angry. Suddenly she laughed and said, "How nice! My old one is almost worn out." Yes, Cindy and she had been very good friends. It just wasn't the same after Kim moved in and spoiled it all.

As Tommy left for the party, he said, "You can ride my bike if you want. But don't wreck it."

Terry looked for the chapter where Beth dies. But even that wasn't miserable enough to suit her mood. She imagined instead that Jo had died and all the others, Beth included, were standing around her grave weeping. She would have cried herself except that her mother was watching her every little while, as she gathered up clothes to wash, and smiling because Terry was reading a girl's book.

Terry thought she couldn't stand it if her mother smiled at her once more, the way she felt. "I'm going out," she said.

"Be back in time for supper," her mother replied.

Terry went down to the basement and hauled Tommy's bike up the steps. Perhaps her legs had stretched since she last tried to ride it. No, blast it, they weren't any longer. Now she'd have sore toes again from riding the bike.

She could at least ride past Cindy's house and see if she and Kim were around, she decided as she rode shakily along the sidewalk by the woods. But when she came to the corner, instead of turning, the bike went straight on across the street to Greg's house.

What were they doing now, she wondered. Dared she look in the window and see?

The windows were open and she could hear the boys laughing and shouting inside. She held onto a sill and jumped, but she couldn't get a long enough look to see what was going on. Leaning the bike against the house, she managed to get one knee onto the seat, and looked in the window.

The boys were hopping, one shoe on and one shoe off, kicking peanuts across the room with their stocking feet. Their hands were clasped behind their backs, but they used their elbows for joggling each other.

Tommy had just knocked Greg off balance. Greg was dressed as a cowboy. Mike was trying to find his peanut, which was covered up by his ghost costume. Danny had rolled up the sleeves of his football uniform, but still he looked hot. Terry remembered how Danny had sold Christmas cards all over town the year before to earn money for the uniform. In the corner stood Mr. Zimmer, urging them on.

Danny made it to the other side of the room.

"You win, Danny," Mr. Zimmer said, handing him a jackknife for a prize.

"That'll come in handy when we build the tree house," Greg said.

"What tree house?" Mrs. Zimmer asked, coming in from the kitchen. She was facing the window, and Terry ducked quickly.

Mr. Zimmer said, "I've been telling the fellows about the tree house I had when I was a boy. A clubhouse, actually. All the boys on the block were members." He laughed. "I remember we spent most of our time chasing the girls away. We had a lot of fun with that tree house."

"We're going to have a boys' club too," Tommy said. "After we eat, we're going to draw up plans for the tree house."

Terry couldn't hold her cramped position any longer. Quietly she climbed down and wheeled the bike home.

After putting the bike away in the basement, Terry wondered what to do next. If she could only find a quiet place to cry in.

She was in luck. The washroom was empty. Terry climbed into a laundry tub and leaned back. But she couldn't make the tears come. She thought about running away. That would solve everything. But the trouble was, there was no place to run to.

That reminded her of the only time she had really run away. She had been six or seven. Now she didn't know why she had been so angry. But she remembered walking down dark streets, wanting to go home. And being terrified when she heard footsteps behind her, following her. She had turned around, and there was her mother.

"You didn't think I'd let you go out after dark alone?" her mother had said.

Terry sighed. Life had been so much simpler then. Now there was nothing for her to do but to go upstairs to a dreary supper and finish out the day.

Her mother had already started supper.

"Oh, frankfurters," Terry said. The only way she liked them was in rolls, but her mother never made them that way. And then she spied a package of rolls, "Hey, hot dogs!" she exclaimed.

"Yes," said her mother. "Like a picnic. An indoor one. You can have as many as you can eat. And there's potato salad too." She boiled the frankfurters and then fried them crisply, burned the way Terry liked them.

"I thought about having a real picnic," her mother added as she put the food on the table. "But the ironing was so far behind and there was so much to do, I just didn't see how I could take the time."

After wolfing down four hot dogs and a good deal of potato salad, Terry had that happy full feeling she had at Christmas and Easter.

Since it was a holiday, Terry didn't have to help with the dishes. But she figured she might just as well, to kill time. Afterward her mother said, "We could go up on the roof and try to see the fireworks from the park. Or maybe you'd rather burn some sparklers yourself."

"We don't have any sparklers," Terry said, thinking disgustedly that her mother was making fun of her.

"Well, not exactly," her mother agreed. "But one of the girls — women, I mean — at work was telling me that scouring pads, the kind without soap in them, can be used as sparklers. You stretch a wire hanger

91

out straight and fasten the pad to the end with wire."

Scouring pads, Terry discovered, did make good sparklers. She burned them, holding the wire well away from her because the sparks flew in all directions, while her mother watched and gossiped with some of the neighbors.

Terry decided she was going to get even with those boys somehow. With her sparkler, she wrote out, "I hate boys," and looked to see if her mother could read it. Hate was a word she wasn't allowed to use. But her mother was busy listening to something Mrs. Pinehurst was saying.

Tree Houses Are for Boys

"**W**HO WANTS to be in your old club anyway,"
Terry said when her brother told her about the pro-
posed boys' club. "It sounds dumb, a club with just
boys in it."

Tommy wasn't fooled. "I can't help it," he said.
"What other kind is there but boys' clubs and girls'
clubs? Does the Camp Fire Girls let boys join?"

Terry wasn't sure a boy had ever *tried* to join the
Camp Fire Girls, but she didn't think that argument
would get her anywhere. "Well, you can't use my tree
for the tree house," she said. The club was bad
enough but they wanted to take her tree away too.
She walked slower. They were on their way to see the
new plans Mr. Zimmer had drawn up for the tree

house. Now Terry wasn't sure she wanted to go. But she didn't want to stay away either.

"It's the only tree Greg's father can get up in," Tommy protested. "And he says it has two branches just right for the tree house. After all, he's supplying everything. You can help build it if you want. And you can go in it whenever we aren't having a meeting."

Mr. Zimmer was at work. He was a foreman for a tool manufacturer. But Greg had the plans spread out on the dining room table. The tree house in the sketch had walls on two sides and a flat roof, with a ladder going all the way up to the top so the roof could be used as well.

They all agreed they were fine plans, and they were anxious to get started building. But not so Mr. Zimmer. Every day he had new plans ready. He read books on housebuilding and consulted friends of his in the construction business.

"It would be nice to have it all walled in for cold days," he said. "That means we'll have to put a door in here. And a flat roof wouldn't shuck off the rain the way a ridged one would."

Next came windows. And a chimney so they could have a stove to warm up the place in winter. It began, on paper, to look like a miniature house.

Although the boys enjoyed listening to Mr. Zimmer's grand plans, they grew more impatient each day. "Even if he ever finishes making plans," Mike said one day, "it'll take us years to build that thing."

94

"Don't worry," Greg said. "Mom says he's bound to lose interest pretty soon."

When at last they were ready to start building, Terry was hoping the boys would forget about their club by the time the tree house was finished.

Mr. Zimmer let the gang do all the work, but he wanted to be there to tell them what to do. This meant that they could only work on it for a little while each day after supper. Terry couldn't go until after she was through drying dishes, and her mother wasn't especially keen on letting her go then.

"Tree houses are for boys," Mrs. Seth said. "Perhaps Mr. Zimmer would let you have some leftover pieces and you and Cindy and Kim could make a puppet theater." Terry made no reply and her mother sighed. Terry didn't say anything about the boys' club. She knew what her mother would think of that.

After the heavy timbers for the foundation were in place and the ladder added, Terry was allowed to help nail the floor down. Mr. Zimmer was as strict with her as with the others. If a nail wasn't in straight, she had to pull it up and try again.

On the day they finished the floor, Mr. Zimmer said, "Fellows, I'm sorry, but I won't be able to help you for a while. Mrs. Zimmer has been after me to make her an extra kitchen cabinet for some time. Now it seems she's in an awful hurry for it. I'll leave the plans with Greg, and if you run into any trouble, you be sure to let me know."

Greg turned his back so his father wouldn't see him grinning. He had had a long talk with his mother that afternoon.

"Gee, that's too bad," Tommy said. The others tried to look as disappointed as possible.

"Well, good luck," Mr. Zimmer said sadly as he walked away.

"Thanks a lot," Tommy called after him. "Yeah, thanks," the others chorused.

As soon as he was out of hearing, Mike said, "This is all the tree house we need. Who cares about the other junk?" They all agreed.

The next morning Terry didn't wake up until Tommy returned from his paper route. He threw his bag inside and slammed the door on his way out. It wasn't like him to slam doors. He must be in a hurry to get to the tree house, she thought. So was she. Gulping down her cereal, she left the dirty dishes for later and hurried to the woods.

She heard voices from the tree house and stopped in horror. They were electing officers. Tommy was president. Greg was elected vice president. Mike was chosen as secretary.

"And now we'll vote for treasurer," Tommy said.

"Treasurer of what?" Danny yelped. "You mean we gotta pay dues?"

"We can decide that later," Tommy said. "But we have to have a treasurer."

Gravely they elected Danny to that office. "Isn't

that stupid?" Terry thought to herself. "There's only one person left and they have to vote on it."

The boys saw her and fell silent. As she drew nearer, Tommy said, "We're having a meeting."

"So what?" Terry said. "I'm just walking through. Anybody's got a right to walk through."

And walk through she did, since she had said it. Past the open space in the middle of the woods where the weeds were as tall as Soupy, through some more trees, and out on the other side.

"You'd think they'd want somebody in the club who wasn't an officer," Terry thought. Well, she'd show them somehow. She didn't know how at the moment. In the meantime here she was near Cindy's house.

Cindy had always been a good friend. Maybe she wasn't even mad at Terry for ignoring her so long. Anyway, she wasn't one to stay mad for long. All at once Terry wanted very badly to see her friend again. If she was lucky, maybe Kim wouldn't be there.

There was no one in Cindy's yard or in Kim's. Terry rang Cindy's doorbell.

Mrs. Ford came to the door. "Hello, Terry," she said. "It's good to see you again. But I'm afraid Cindy isn't home. She and Kim are out on their bicycles somewhere." She smiled at Terry. "But you come back this afternoon. I know they would be glad to see you."

Terry went home for lunch. Tommy came in while

she was finishing her sandwich. He said "Hi," but Terry ignored him. She went outside so he couldn't say anything more.

Danny and Mike came out after her. Terry looked right through them.

The two boys walked toward the woods with their noses in the air. "Kalamazoo," Terry heard Mike say. "Chattanooga," his brother replied. "Shhh," Mike said. They both laughed.

In another minute Tommy came out. Smiling mysteriously, he said, "Hi, Terry. Kalamazoo."

"Chattanooga," Terry said to the bricks on the apartment wall.

"Who told you the answer to the password?" Tommy said angrily. "Nobody would have told you. You've been spying on us. Now we'll have to get another password. I'm warning you, you stay away from the tree house when we're having meetings."

"I really couldn't care less about your silly old passwords," Terry said airily.

Tommy stalked off. Terry considered hiding in the woods by the tree house, trying to find out the new password. But they would probably be watching for her.

She sat glumly on the front step wishing Soupy didn't have to stay so long at his grandmother's. He had looked so sad when he said good-by to her. She hadn't realized how much she would miss him.

Terry continued staring at the sidewalk and didn't hear anyone approach. Suddenly Cindy was standing, scowling, in front of her. Terry looked up and saw Kim on the opposite corner.

"Oh, hi, Cindy," Terry said, smiling tentatively. "Why is Kim waiting there?"

"Because you're mad at her," Cindy said belligerently. "She never did anything to you and you're mad at her."

"No, I'm not," Terry said, embarrassed. "I never said I was."

"You act like it," Cindy said. "Ever since she moved in, you don't come up to play anymore."

"Well, you never come here," Terry said defensively, although she had just realized it. "Why should I always have to go to your place?"

"You hardly ever said I should come to your apartment. I thought you didn't want me to. I'm always asking you to come to my place," Cindy said. "Kim and I have looked around for you lots of times. The few times we found you, you said you were busy."

Terry didn't know why she hadn't invited her friend over more. Except that Cindy had a house with a room of her own and a yard where it was fun to play. Cindy could even have Terry stay over for supper without asking her mother a day ahead of time. Terry had slept at Cindy's a few times too. Mrs. Seth didn't want her to do it too often because it was an invitation she couldn't return.

"I'm not mad at Kim," Terry said slowly. "It's just that — we had so much fun before she moved in."

"Well, why can't three play?" Cindy asked.

Terry looked away and shrugged. She didn't know why she had acted so stupidly. All this time she could have had fun playing with Cindy and Kim. It was nice playing with the boys, but they weren't really friends. She was lucky to have a friend like Cindy. Anyone else would have forgotten her by now, or never forgiven her for what she did.

"We could do something now," Terry mumbled, clearing her throat. "Kim, too, I mean."

Cindy waved to Kim to come. Terry wondered what she could say to her.

But Kim spoke first. "How come you're not in that tree house with those boys?" she asked.

Terry explained about the boys' club.

"I think that's real mean," Kim said. "Maybe we can do something to get back at them." Why hadn't she ever even tried to like Kim, Terry wondered.

They tried to think of things to do to the boys but couldn't come up with anything worthwhile.

"Let's do something while we're thinking," Cindy said.

"Cindy says you always think of wonderful things to do, Terry," said Kim.

Terry glowed. But now she'd have to think of something quickly. "Why don't we, uh — hey, remember last summer, Cindy, when we made rooms out of the weeds in the woods and played house there? The weeds are tall enough now and nobody's knocked them down yet," she said.

101

Cindy and Kim liked the idea, and they trampled down rooms in the weeds.

"You know what we could do tomorrow?" Kim said as they parted. "We could take a long hike on our bikes."

"Let's not," Cindy said quickly, glancing at Terry. "We did that today."

Terry glared at Kim, who was looking puzzled. Maybe she doesn't know, Terry thought. She tried to think of something exciting to do the next day. Suddenly a beautiful idea came to her. "I know what we can do if we get up early enough," she said. She told the girls her plan.

Terry arrived home smiling happily. Her mother would be so pleased to learn she had been with Cindy and Kim. And tomorrow she would get even with the boys.

Mrs. Seth was setting the table. Before Terry could say a word, she said, "The breakfast dishes aren't done yet."

Terry remembered that she had been in too much of a hurry to do them in the morning. Later she had completely forgotten them. Her mother sounded sad and tired, not angry. Terry wished that her mother would yell at her and get it over with.

"Perhaps you should do the dishes by yourself tonight as punishment," Mrs. Seth said. Why couldn't her mother just tell her what her punishment was instead of suggesting it, as if Terry had a chance to say no?

After supper Terry did the dishes while her mother darned socks.

"Terry, do you think I ask too much of you?" Mrs. Seth asked.

Oh, gosh, was she never going to hear the end of it? Terry wondered. She didn't forget the dishes very often. She hoped her mother wasn't going to start in on, "When I was your age," and how responsible she was then. Perhaps she could convince her mother that she was hopeless and nothing could be done about it. It would avoid so much trouble for both of them.

"No, I guess not," she answered her mother's question, rubbing at a knife so hard that she cut through the dishcloth.

Mrs. Seth went on with her work without looking up. "The reason I ask," she said, "is because I was hoping I could ask even more of you. I would like to work overtime next week and the week after. But I can't do it unless you take over in the evening, make supper, and clean up afterwards."

"Oh, no!" Terry cried. At her mother's surprised stare, she added hastily, "Of course I'll help. But I thought you hated to work overtime." Mrs. Seth could work late hours any time in the summer, when a lot of the workers were on vacation. But she always said it was more important to be home with her children than to make extra money. They must really be in trouble, Terry thought.

Terry delved behind the cups in the cupboard and took out her bicycle money. "Would this help?" Often she had wanted to spend her money, figuring she would never have enough for a bike. She was glad now that her mother hadn't let her spend it.

"Thank you," her mother said, smiling. "You put it back for now. I'll use it if I have to."

Terry finished the dishes in a daze, trying to think of ways to make money. There wasn't anything she could sell. Her mother wouldn't let her sell Christmas cards even if it were the season for it. She wasn't allowed to baby-sit either.

"I bet Tommy would let you have his money," Terry said, flinging the dishtowel on its rod.

"I know," Mrs. Seth said, taking out the mop to clean up the puddle of water Terry had spilled on the floor. "But he already buys some of his own clothes. I want him to keep the rest. He works hard for it." Terry's mother finished mopping and started filling up the sink again.

"What are you doing?" Terry asked.

"The pots and pans don't wash themselves," her mother said. There they were, on the stove next to the sink, where Terry had overlooked them. Mrs. Seth picked up the dishcloth and saw the hole in it.

The explosion Terry waited for didn't come. The silence was even worse. Her mother must already have decided that she was hopeless. What was the use of trying any more? Terry wandered into the other room and stood by the window, holding her breath to keep back the tears. She didn't hear her mother say pleasantly, "I should really make you do this. But you'll have enough to do when I'm working overtime."

Terry was so depressed that she forgot to ask her mother to awaken her the next morning. But Cindy phoned, just in case, soon after Tommy had left.

"I'll call Kim now," Cindy said. "See you at the tree house."

Terry ate, dressed, slopped soapy water around in the dishes, rinsed them and left them to dry, and folded the blankets. Why did they go every which way when she was in a hurry? Then she ran out to the tree house. Cindy and Kim were already there.

Now all they had to do was wait for the boys to show up. After all, Tommy had said she could use the tree house when the boys weren't having a meeting. The boys weren't going to have a meeting today. Not unless they dragged the girls from the tree house, or surrendered. The term of surrender Terry had in mind was letting the girls into the boys' club.

"Look in the box," Kim told Terry, pointing to a cardboard box with the words *See the world-famous bug zoo. 1¢ a look* painted on it. Inside were jars and jars, the tops covered with wax paper with holes punched in it, held on by elastic bands.

Terry lifted out each jar and examined it. They held grasshoppers, caterpillars, ants, flies, worms, and even a bumblebee, each with a leaf to nibble on. She was hurt that Tommy hadn't mentioned the zoo to her. It would have been fun to help collect the bugs. Except for the bumblebee. She admitted to herself that she missed playing with the boys something

105

awful. Why couldn't she play with Cindy and Kim and with the boys as well?

"It sure is a nice collection," she said. The boys would be good and mad if they let the bugs go. But that would be too mean a thing to do.

It seemed a long wait before the boys came.

"Hi," Tommy said agreeably. "Did you see the zoo? How do you like it?"

"Neat," Terry told him reluctantly. Cindy and Kim smiled nervously and waited for the fireworks.

"It was," Greg said. "But we have to bust it up. My mom wants the jars back for canning. Boy, was she mad when she found them gone."

"You can't find something gone," Tommy said. "If you find it, it isn't gone any more."

"Smart, real smart," Greg said scornfully. "Hey, Terry, will you shove the box down? We'll catch it."

"Yeah, you girls can stay up there till we return the jars. Then you'll have to go because we're going to have a meeting," Tommy said.

"We're not going anywhere," Terry told him, making no move to give them the box. "I have as much right here as you have. We're going to stay up here all day."

The effect was disappointing. Tommy whispered to the others and said, "Go ahead. We can have a meeting somewhere else. Just hand the box down and we'll leave you alone."

Terry thought desperately. And a beautiful idea came to her. "Come and get it," she said. Greg started up the ladder. "Of course, if you do — " Greg stopped. "It means you've joined our club." She hoped Cindy and Kim wouldn't say, "What club?" They didn't.

"Because that's how you get invitationed into our club, by coming up when we're having a meeting," Terry went on. "It's a girls' club," she added for good measure.

"I think she means initiated," Tommy said as Greg jumped off the ladder. "She can't speak English yet." Still, he gave her a look and a nod that meant he admired her trick.

"Listen, I gotta have those jars," Greg said. "Mom's furious."

"Too, too bad," Terry said coolly. "Go shrink your head in acid." Cindy looked at her oddly. Her friend never talked like that, Terry realized, and neither had she until she had started being with the boys so much.

Greg gave up. "C'mon, you guys," he said. "I'll go tell my mother I can't get the jars back."

When she saw her plan wasn't working, Terry relented. The girls handed down the box and watched the boys walk away with it.

"We don't have a club," Kim said.

"We do now," Cindy said, familiar with Terry's method of non-lying. "It's a shame, Terry. It was a good idea."

"Why don't we go to my house?" Kim said. "I have to clean my room anyhow. My mother almost didn't let me out this morning because I was supposed to do it yesterday."

"Wait a minute. Let me think," Terry said. She leaned against the tree trunk and cupped her chin in her hands and thought. Her second plan had been good. Greg had been plenty annoyed.

"Listen," she said excitedly. "They'll probably come back here to see if we've gone. What if they think we have when we haven't? If we all get back here by the trunk, they can't see us from below."

They all crouched down at the back of the tree house and waited. After a while they grew restless. Perhaps the boys had decided to stay at Greg's.

Terry was on the point of giving it up when they heard Danny say, "It's O.K. They're not here."

Tommy came up first. He stared at them open-mouthed, too surprised to speak. The other boys shoved him aside as they climbed up.

"Welcome to the girls' club," Terry said sweetly.

"That's not fair," Greg said angrily. "You don't have to join a club if you don't want to."

"We decline to be invitationed," Tommy said. "But thanks just the same."

"I can't wait till school starts," Kim said dreamily, "so we can tell all the kids."

A heavy silence fell. The boys looked at each other uneasily.

A friend in need, Terry thought. She smiled gratefully at Kim. Then she thrust the knife in deeper. "Why don't you go home now and tell your big brother about it? Steve knows a lot of the guys at school, doesn't he?"

"Hold it, just hold it a minute," Tommy said anxiously. "What do you want from us?"

Terry appeared to think things over. Then she said slowly, "Since you don't really want to join our club, we might be willing to join yours instead. What do you think?" she asked the girls.

"I guess so," Kim said. Cindy nodded. She didn't dare speak because she knew she'd burst out laughing.

Greg snapped his fingers. "Say, you know what Mom said when we told her what a hard time we had getting the jars? I thought it was a crazy idea, but maybe — "

"Let's have a conference," Tommy said. The boys climbed down and went into a huddle a little distance away.

They came back and stood beneath the tree. "We're willing to compromise," Tommy said. "You can be in our club, in the ladies' auxiliary. You can come to the meetings we have for the whole club. But you have to let us have the tree house when we have our own meetings. And you can have meetings of your own without telling us."

"And you have to stop saying we're in your club," Greg demanded.

Terry turned to the girls. "It's probably the best we can do," she said, low enough so the boys wouldn't hear. "It's better than nothing." She didn't like being called a lady, but still it was a way of getting into the boys' club.

Having gotten what they wanted, the girls went to Kim's and spent the rest of the day there.

That evening Mrs. Seth brightened as Terry told her she had been playing with Cindy and Kim. But as Terry went on to relate her morning's adventures, Mrs. Seth frowned.

"I might have known," she said. "Now that you're back playing with the girls, you're trying to make tomboys out of them."

Wish Before Blowing

ON HER WAY UPSTAIRS for lunch, Terry glanced at the mail table near the front door. It was used for mail too large for the boxes and today it was piled high with thick catalogs.

She shuffled through them until she found the one addressed to her mother and took it upstairs. But before she settled down with it, there was something she meant to do. What was it? Oh, yes, the eggs.

Today was her first day of cooking supper. Her mother told her to make scrambled eggs, because Terry knew how, and sausages, because they were easy. Terry said nothing, but she liked her eggs hard-boiled and that was how she intended to have them. She had decided to cook them while she was home for lunch so they would be cold by suppertime.

She put two eggs in a pan of water and put a match to the burner, standing well away from it as her mother had showed her long ago. Then she slapped some apple jelly on bread and sprawled on the floor in the other room with the catalog. "Remember," she told herself, "wipe up the crumbs so she doesn't know I've been eating in here."

Bicycles first. She sighed. The lowest priced one was an unreachable thirty dollars. She had $8.57 now because Tommy had paid her for helping him with his route a couple of times. How close was she? Did she divide eight by thirty or thirty by eight? Soon the catalog page was covered with figures and still she had no idea.

Well, she could subtract. That gave her almost $21.50 to go. That was clear enough. It was too far.

Next to her own bicycle was a funny bicycle built for two. There was no limit to the marvelous things to be found in the catalog. When Terry was ill, her mother always brought out the catalog, along with the awful hot lemonade and the senna tea.

Terry browsed next. On another page she found a spirit duplicator, which sounded fascinating. It turned out to have something to do with printing.

And here was a winch. She'd always thought that was an English lady. But it was a machine that rope was not included with. There were tree planters with a lot of little pots on them. They didn't look strong enough for trees. Where would the roots go?

Monkeys. She could have a monkey for a few dollars more than her bicycle. Her mother would probably say no, though. Or else the landlord would. Cats were allowed but not dogs. So maybe monkeys were out.

The rocking lounger certainly looked comfortable. That would be nice for her mother when she was especially tired. Someday she would buy her mother one. And a house. And an electric dishwasher. Did they dry dishes too? Yes, they did.

Maybe she should buy her mother a guitar. Her mother never seemed to have much fun. She didn't even like to ride on Ferris wheels. It must be awful to be a grownup and not like anything anymore.

Here were the girls' clothes, the section Terry used to make paper dolls from. Once her mother had been awfully mad, because she had cut it apart before she'd seen it.

Usually dresses didn't interest Terry. They were something to throw on for school or church. But once in a while she saw a dress that took her breath away. She saw one now. It had a gray and blue and red plaid full-skirted jumper over a bright red dress. The dress had ruffles on the elbow-length sleeves.

But it was $6.98. That was an awful lot for one dress. What was she worried about? Her birthday was coming in a couple of weeks. She was sure her mother would spend a little extra for a dress.

Her heart sank. Her mother wasn't working overtime for the fun of it. Terry scolded herself for think-ing about presents when she should be thinking of ways to help her mother. Maybe she wouldn't even get a present. She shouldn't expect one.

What she should really do was tell her mother not to buy one. And say it as though she meant it. That wouldn't be easy, but she could practice up first.

Anyway, if her mother didn't need her bike money, Terry could buy the dress with it. Her mother couldn't object to that. As soon as her mother was through working overtime, she would ask her.

Suddenly she was aware of a heavy pounding on the door. "Terry, are you there?" Cindy called.

Terry ran to the door. Cindy and Kim were there, looking anxious.

"We thought you were dead," Kim said. "We've been tapping and tapping. What happened to you? You said you'd meet us. It's been over an hour."

"It can't be," Terry said. "I just got here."

WHAM! An explosion sounded from the other room.

"What was that!" Cindy shrieked.

"Gosh, it sounded like a rifle," Terry said. At least, it sounded like the rifles on TV. "I better see what it is," she said bravely, her heart pounding.

The three of them crowded through the doorway.

"Phew, what a smell!" Kim exclaimed.

Cindy rushed to open the window but it was al-ready open.

"My eggs," Terry moaned as an eggshell crunched under her foot. "My hard boiled eggs. They're all over the place."

There were pieces of egg and eggshell on the stove, in the sink, on the floor.

"We'll practically have to take the stove apart to get it clean," Cindy said.

They set to work, sweeping and scrubbing, and soon had things to rights. Except that the pan the eggs were in would probably never look the same again.

Terry was worried that things would continue the way they had started. But that evening supper went smoothly, although eggs were the last thing she wanted. And she wished she hadn't burned the sausages quite so much because it made the frying pan difficult to clean.

"That wasn't too bad," Tommy said as he dried the dishes.

Terry was glad he had to help, but she wished he'd put the dishes away in the right places. After he was through, she had to straighten out the cupboard.

At last the first day's work was over. Her mother came home looking a little tired, but she smiled on seeing her kitchen in good order.

Terry waited to be praised. She was amazed herself at the good job she had done, except for the exploding eggs.

But all her mother said was, "Well, just as I expected. You see, there's nothing to it."

Terry scowled. Was that all her reward for trying so hard? Nothing to it, my foot, she thought.

"I guess I'm not much good at making jokes when I'm tired," her mother said. "I did mean it nicely, Terry."

"Oh," Terry said, brightening. She wished her mother would ring a bell or something when she made a joke.

The days went by quickly. Sometimes Terry felt like complaining about the extra work. Dishes broke, food was burned or underdone, once she put too much salt in the potatoes. Now and then Tommy made a face over his meal but he said nothing.

Yet she didn't have the heart to complain. Each night her mother looked more tired. It was in her eyes especially that Terry noticed it. They no longer seemed able to look straight through her and see everything she'd been up to.

On Saturday of the first week Terry was free to do whatever she chose. But her mother looked so weary that Terry begged to be allowed to help hang up the wash.

"If you're sure you want to," her mother said. "Then I can get to the store earlier than I'd planned."

Her mother carried the heavy clothes basket out. They bent and stretched, bent and stretched, hanging the clothes, until Terry began to feel like a yoyo. She didn't think much of the system. There must be a better way.

And a better idea came to her. Holding all the wet

wash she could manage on one arm, she slung things one by one over the line. Her mother followed close behind her and pinned them. It saved a lot of time and her mother was pleased at not having to do any bending. Terry wondered if there were some way she could sell the idea. There might be a fortune in it.

While they were working, Terry told her mother about the dress in the catalog she'd like to buy some day. Her mother said she would take a look at it.

"By the way," Mrs. Seth said, "don't forget to invite Cindy and Kim and Soupy to your birthday party. You haven't said a thing about your birthday. Did you forget it was coming?"

"No, I didn't forget," Terry said. "I don't need a party. Or any presents either." She tried to say it as though she were looking forward to skipping her birthday, but it came out sort of miserable.

Her mother couldn't help laughing and Terry didn't blame her. "We'll manage something," Mrs. Seth said. "You know, Terry, lately I've been so pleased with—"

She didn't finish. Just then Terry reached in for the last of the wash, putting one foot on the edge of the basket. The basket tipped and the contents and Terry tumbled into the dirt together.

"I'm sorry," Terry said, getting to her feet.

"I know," her mother said resignedly. "Run along now and let me finish this. You've been helping all week. Enough is enough."

She had worked hard all week, Terry thought. But

her mother had worked even harder. Still, going away seemed the best thing she could do right now. She walked slowly to Cindy's. On the way she found a caterpillar and stroked the furry wriggling animal, wishing she could trade places with it. "All you have to do is slither around till it's time to turn into a butterfly," she told it bitterly.

But as often happened when she felt miserable, Terry soon had something to feel more miserable about.

Cindy and Kim couldn't come to her party. They were both going to camp for a week, starting the day before her birthday.

"But why do you have to go then?" Terry asked.

"I'm sorry, Terry. Kim signed up long ago. She didn't know it was your birthday. She asked me if I wanted to go. You weren't playing with us then, so I figured that week was as good as any other," Cindy said.

"We've been meaning to tell you, but somehow we just never got it out," Kim said. "And you can't change the time at the camp or get your money back if you don't go. You aren't mad, are you, Terry?"

"No, I'm not mad," Terry said. "It just happened, I guess."

"Maybe you could have the party some other day," Cindy suggested.

"It wouldn't be the same," Terry said.

And she stuck to that. Her mother and Tommy both

118

insisted she have it earlier or later, but she refused. If she couldn't have a birthday party on her birthday, she didn't want one.

Soupy came home the next day and told Terry all about his visit at least a dozen times, pausing now and then to ask, "Did you miss me?" Terry assured him she had.

Terry's second week of cooking went easier. She avoided some of the mistakes of the first week. But she was glad to see Saturday come. It wasn't the work she minded so much as her mother's tiredness. Her mother was too tired even to be cross. It made Terry uneasy. She hoped whatever trouble they were in was over now.

But instead of resting on Saturday, Mrs. Seth went downtown shopping and was gone most of the day.

Terry and Soupy went to say good-bye to Cindy and Kim, who were leaving for camp early the next afternoon. On the way Soupy said, "I could come to your birtday, Terry. If you wanted me to. I'm not asting. Daddy said not to ast."

"Soupy, of course you're coming. You always do. I told you to, didn't I?" Terry replied.

"No you dint," Soupy said sadly.

Terry mentally kicked herself. What a stupid thing to forget. "You're silly," she said. "I wouldn't think of not having you. We won't exactly have a party, but you come for supper and we'll think of something fun to do."

"That's good," Soupy said, " 'cause Daddy got you a present way from Mishtigen. You want to know what it is?"

"You're not allowed to tell," Terry said sharply. What could it be that Mr. O'Halloran had to send for it from Michigan? She wished Soupy was a little bit older so she could wheedle it out of him honorably.

They found Cindy and Kim packing Kim's things in her room. Cindy was already packed. Awkwardly they talked for a while about nothing in particular.

Suddenly Kim exclaimed, "I wish you were going with us, Terry."

"We'll write to you, honest," Cindy said.

It would be nice to get a letter, Terry thought.

Before she left, Kim and Cindy each gave her a present. Terry felt them on the way home. Kim's was a shapeless lump. Cindy's was flat and oblong. A good sign. And the paper gave on three sides. That clinched it—it was a book. Maybe it was a Nancy Drew.

She had to wait all through Sunday to find out. But she didn't have to wait long on Monday, her birthday.

A heavy pounding awakened her and she opened her eyes as her mother went to the door. There was Soupy, in his pajamas, with some kind of plant in his hands.

"Soupy, do you know what time it is?" Mrs. Seth asked. "Terry isn't even awake yet."

"Yes, I am," Terry said, jumping out of bed.

"You might as well stay for breakfast," Mrs. Seth

told Soupy. "I don't suppose your father knows you're here?"

"He's still asleep," Soupy said. "He dint say I couldn't come."

Soupy gave Terry the plant. "It's got a card on it," he said.

The card was as large as the plant. It was typed, but Soupy had signed his name.

> For Terry, with love,
> from Soupy

She had taught him that the day he came home from kindergarten crying bitterly because they made him write Kevin instead of his "real" name. His father always called him Kevin so the name wouldn't seem completely strange to him, but Soupy preferred the other.

After admiring the card, Terry turned to the plant. She couldn't believe her eyes. It looked like a miniature rosebush. There were several buds with one tiny pink flower and lots of dainty little leaves.

She felt one of the tiny buds.

"Ouch!" she cried. It had to be a rosebush. It had thorns.

She threw her arms around Soupy and hugged him. "It's a wonderful present. Isn't it, Mom?"

"It certainly is," Mrs. Seth said. "I never saw anything like it. But I have to hurry now. You and Soupy sit down, your cereal is ready. Tommy, time to get up."

121

For Terry, with love,
from SOLPY

Tommy threshed around a few times, knocked his pillow on the floor, and fell on the floor himself when he tried to pick it up. He leaped to his feet, splashed cold water on his face at the sink, and he was ready to face the day. He joined his sister and Soupy at the table while Mrs. Seth prepared to leave.

"You can open the presents you have, but can you wait for tonight for the rest, Terry?" her mother asked.

"Sure," Terry said.

"All right. Come and get your birthday greeting," said her mother.

Terry received a kiss and a spank. "Take whichever shoe fits," her mother said. They both laughed. This was a yearly ritual.

Mrs. Seth left for work, saying she would be home as soon as possible. Terry went back to her breakfast.

"A-ee er-ay," Tommy said with his mouth full.

Terry opened her presents from Cindy and Kim while she ate. The book from Cindy was *Mrs. Wiggs of the Cabbage Patch*. It wasn't a title that she would reach for on a library shelf, but Cindy must have had a reason. At any rate, Terry wasn't about to dislike a book that was hers to keep.

Kim's gift was a china porcupine full of toothpick quills.

"What's it for?" Tommy asked.

"I dunno. Hey, look, the toothpicks come out," Terry said. "Let's take 'em all out and put 'em in again."

"Sounds real exciting, but I gotta get dressed and go," Tommy said on his way into the other room.

Terry let Soupy play with her porcupine while she studied her rosebush.

"I know somethin' I can't tell," Soupy said.

"What is it? You can tell me, can't you?" Terry coaxed, wondering what he was up to.

Soupy watched her out of the corner of his eyes. "Nope, can't," he said. "But it's about a birtday."

"My birthday?" Maybe he had another surprise for her.

"Nope," Soupy said, still watching her.

Suddenly Terry caught on. "I know your birthday's coming in a couple weeks. Anyhow, you could have told me that right out."

"Daddy said I can't remine people on account of the presents. Daddy says people should give presents 'cause they want to, not 'cause I remine them," Soupy announced virtuously.

Terry decided she would get something very nice for Soupy's birthday. She didn't know exactly what, but she would still have enough money after buying her dress.

"Soupy, you want to see my bike money?" she said, groping around for it in the cupboard. She looked on the shelf where she remembered putting it, on the shelf above and the shelf below.

"Tommy!" she yelled in a panic. "My money's gone!"

Her brother didn't seem concerned. He came in to get his paper bag and told her not to worry about it.

"Maybe you put it some place else and forgot," he said.

"Forgot where I put nearly ten dollars?" she shrieked, but Tommy was gone.

Something was going on. If Tommy wasn't alarmed about the money, it meant he knew where it was and didn't want to say. But he wouldn't take it. The only thing she could think of was that her mother might have needed the money and was too embarrassed to say so. That didn't make much sense. She gave up thinking about it.

"Go get dressed, Soupy. I'll meet you outside," she said.

They played together all morning. It was dull without Cindy and Kim, and she was afraid the boys would chase them away.

After an early lunch at Soupy's, they went out to the treehouse with Mrs. Wiggs. Soupy loved to be read to; he didn't care what sort of book it was.

The story wasn't nearly as bad as the title sounded. Mrs. Wiggs had a bunch of children and there were funny happenings and lots of troubles. But the end of Chapter II was disturbing.

". . . and he fearlessly drifted away into the Shadowy Valley where his lost childhood lay," Terry read.

"Now isn't that *mean!*" she exclaimed. "It's one of those places where they don't make out if somebody's dying or dreaming. I hate it when they do that." How was she supposed to know whether to cry or not?

Soupy wasn't any help. Neither was Chapter III. Terry leafed through it and saw it was a lot of garbage about some man and lady, who had nothing to do with the story, having a fight. The story didn't pick up again until the fourth chapter, but Terry didn't allow herself to skip.

She was rescued by the arrival of the boys.

"Sorry, we'll be using the tree house now," Greg said.

"Oh, let 'em stay," Tommy said. "It's Terry's birthday and she isn't even having a party. Besides, we've never had a meeting with the auxiliary present."

None of the others objected. Tommy called the roll, but Greg was lost in thought and didn't answer.

Suddenly Greg ran down the ladder. "Don't anybody go away," he yelled back. "I got me an idea."

"More like he got him a fit," Mike commented.

They waited impatiently. At last Greg was back with a whole graham cracker pie, a pile of dishes, and a knife.

"Mom wanted me to bring forks too, but I told her we didn't need them," he said breathlessly.

Tommy cut the pie while Greg explained. "I knew she had this pie, see, but she said it had to wait for dinner. So when I went back, I said how Terry wasn't having a party and how sad it was and I kept looking at that pie, so what could she do?"

The pie disappeared in a hurry. It tasted much better in handfuls than forkfuls, Terry decided.

When Tommy had to leave for his route, Terry and Soupy went to her apartment to read more about Mrs. Wiggs. They went through the boring chapter and finally got back to the interesting part. It turned out that Jim had died after all. Well, she should have known when she saw that Shadowy Valley was capitalized.

Supper didn't take any time to make because it was all store-bought. Mrs. Seth brought home chicken chow mein, ice cream, and a cake with *Happy Birthday Terry* on it. The rose bush was placed in the center of the table next to the cake, and the eleven candles were lit.

Terry gulped down her chow mein. Her presents would come with the blowing out of the candles. Everyone else seemed to be taking his time.

"Hurry up, Soupy," she whispered.

She stared at the flickering candles and wondered why she didn't feel a year older. Now Tommy was only a year ahead of her. Yesterday he'd been two years older. That was the sort of thing, she felt, that arithmetic should explain but didn't.

Finally Tommy dragged out a package from under his bed. Terry took a deep breath and blew out all the candles. "Did you wish?" her mother asked quickly just as she started to blow. There wasn't any time to think. The best Terry could do was to say silently, "I wish awful things would stop happening to me," as she finished blowing.

The tag on the package said, *For Terry from Mother*. She tore it open. There was a mass of bright red and another of plaid. "My dress!" Terry shouted.

It wasn't a dress. It was yards and yards of material.

"The dress cost too much," her mother explained. "So I thought I'd make one. Saturday I looked all over for a plaid close to the one you wanted. The dress pattern isn't exactly right either, but almost."

"I didn't even know you could make a dress," Terry said in awe.

"Well, I never tried it so I don't know that I can't," her mother replied. "It will probably take me a while so I hope you'll be patient."

"That's O.K.," Terry said. "It's a swell present. Thank you."

All through the cake and ice cream nothing was said about a present from Tommy. He kept looking at his mother and grinning, and she smiled back at him. What was so funny?

The moment they were through eating, Mrs. Seth said, "Let's go see if anyone's using the washing machine. Come on, Terry."

Wash clothes on her birthday? With the dishes still on the table? It was crazy. Crazier still, Tommy wanted to come, too. With Soupy following, they all trooped down to the basement. No one was washing clothes.

"Let's see if any lines are free," Mrs. Seth said. They went into the drying room.

Why didn't her mother want to hang the clothes outside? It didn't look like rain.

It was perfectly obvious that the clothes lines were empty. Yet her mother and brother just stood there, waiting.

Terry looked around. There in a corner were the bikes, Tommy's and the one Mike and Danny shared.

But it looked like there were three bikes. She went closer. One was a red bike with a huge red bow on the handle bars. It was a girl's bike. In fact, it was the one in the catalog.

It couldn't be — There was a note tied to the ribbon. It said, *For Terry, from Mother, Tommy, and Terry.*

"Part of it was your bike money," her mother explained.

Terry still couldn't believe it. How could they buy a bike when they needed money so badly? Then she realized why her mother had worked overtime. Suddenly she burst into tears and ran to her mother.

"For Pete's sake, don't you like it?" Tommy asked in disgust.

"She likes it," his mother said, patting Terry gently.

Terry dried her tears quickly and dragged her bike up the stairs.

"You'd better take your bike and go with her," Mrs. Seth told Tommy. "She might forget to come home."

Soupy and Mrs. Seth followed them outside. Terry mounted her bike and rode off without a backward glance. Tommy raced after her, shifting gears rapidly in trying to catch up to her.

"Terry!" Soupy called forlornly.

"Come inside," Mrs. Seth said. "Terry's in another world just now. I'll tell you a story while I do the dishes."

Terry, pedaling furiously, was still amazed. Come to think of it, she hadn't even asked permission to take the bike out after supper. But her mother hadn't said a word to stop her.

In fact, her mother hadn't yelled at her much at all lately. She must really have decided that Terry couldn't help what she did. But that wasn't a very happy thought.

From far behind, a voice yelled, "Terry, will you slow down a little? Will you look where you're going? T — E — R — R — Y!"

Some racer this bike is, Tommy thought. Can't even keep up with a girl.

Terry Seth Hates Terry Seth

It was worth the gasping for breath, forcing her aching legs to push to the top of the hill so she could glide down the other side, faster and faster, slicing through the air.

Uphill and down, speeding or coasting, Terry rode hour after hour, day after day. She wished she could live on her bike and resented the time spent in eating and sleeping.

While the girls were at camp, she rode with the boys or alone. Cindy and Kim together sent her a note on birch bark and followed it with a postcard each. They were back before Terry realized a week had gone by, and they were almost as excited about her bike as she was.

Cindy and Kim and Terry rode to picnics and to the swimming pool. They explored the neighborhood for miles around. Sometimes Cindy or Kim suggested they stay home for a change. Terry shrugged and said, "You stay if you want. I can ride by myself."

"You sure get enthusiastic about things," Kim said once. But she and Cindy went along good-naturedly.

On the few days it rained Terry caught up with her reading. For the first time she had books overdue at the library and had to borrow money from Tommy to pay the fine. She offered to help him with his route to pay him back, but he told her to forget it. He had just received his bond from the paper and was feeling wealthy.

On a Saturday afternoon Terry came home a little late for supper, as usual lately. Soupy was out front, sitting on the step, watching her ride up.

"Hi, Soup," Terry called gaily.

Soupy screwed up his face angrily and cried, "I hate you, I hate you! I hope you and your old bike drop dead!" He jumped up and ran into the building.

"Soupy!" Terry yelled, but he didn't stop. What's he mad about? she wondered. She'd hardly seen him lately, so what could she have done?

She went in to eat. After supper she would find out what was wrong with Soupy. She couldn't remember his ever being angry with her before. Plenty of times she had yelled at him, but he'd never answered back. The most he did was cry when she scolded him, like the time they had delivered papers together. It gave her a funny feeling to know that Soupy was angry with her.

But her mother kept her in to try on the jumper. Mrs. Seth had been working on it a little while every evening and it was done, all but the hem, which was being pinned now. The dress itself was finished, but Terry wasn't allowed to wear it until the jumper was finished too. And then it would be for special occasions, like church.

Terry's mother hadn't had an easy time making the dress and jumper. First they came out too narrow and then too wide. And when the fit was right, there was a pucker somewhere and a seam had to be re-sewn. Over and over and over Terry went through try-on sessions. Remembering what her mother had said about being patient, she tried to be, even when pins were jabbing into her. It took a long time to make a dress by hand, but Terry hoped it wouldn't go on too much longer.

As soon as she came home from church the next morning, Terry went to Soupy's apartment. Mr. O'Halloran said he wasn't home.

She found Soupy outside. He was on the sidewalk by the woods, pushing something. Going nearer, Terry saw he had a baby carriage in front of him. He was inside the handle, one foot on a wheel bar, using the buggy for a scooter, zigzagging down the block at a fast rate.

"Soupy, did anybody say you could play with that carriage?" she called after him.

A thin wail answered her.

"*Soupy, is there a baby in that thing?*" she shrieked.

A moment later a whistle blew three times. "Kevin, come up here," Mr. O'Halloran ordered.

Soupy stopped and looked back at the building.

"Are you coming or do I have to come out and get you," his father yelled.

His chin set defiantly, Soupy marched back without looking at Terry.

As he walked by, Terry said, "Gosh, Soupy, I didn't mean for him to hear, honest."

"Shut up, stupid," Soupy said and walked on.

Terry ran to the baby carriage and pushed it back to the building. She couldn't think of anything to do for Soupy. Mr. O'Halloran sounded good and mad.

She stood outside Soupy's door and listened. From the howling inside, she knew Mr. O'Halloran wasn't hitting a chair this time. She wanted to wait there until it was over but Tommy came looking for her and told her it was time for dinner.

Terry wasn't particularly hungry, but if she didn't clean her plate, her mother took it for granted she was ill. After that there were dishes to dry. Every minute she wanted to hurry to Soupy. Maybe she could have left sooner if she explained things to her mother. But she knew from past experience that whenever she tried to explain, she twisted up everything.

As she was finishing the dishes, Tommy came back.

"Hurry up, we're going to play football," he said.

"Football! In summer?" she asked.

"It's a cool day," her brother replied impatiently. "Anyhow, Danny hasn't had a chance to play in his uniform yet."

"Football isn't a girl's game," Mrs. Seth said, frowning.

"But she *has* to be the center," Tommy said. "There's only two of us on each side."

A year ago Terry had been happy to be the center. Now she knew she had never really taken part in the game. She gave the ball to the runner on either team, watched for cars, and helped keep track of the score. They never let her run with the ball or even punt it. On the other hand, they couldn't very well play without her. It would make the game too one-sided if the side with the ball had to waste half its team as a center. And they'd probably all get run over.

"All right, I'll come," Terry said. Soupy was sure to come out to watch and she could have a talk with him.

"Put your jeans on first. And try to stay clean. Remember, it's Sunday," her mother said.

Terry changed quickly and went outside. The game had barely started when Mr. O'Halloran came out and asked if any of them had seen Soupy. No one had.

"I shouldn't have hit him so hard," Mr. O'Halloran said, "but he's been acting impossible lately. He said he was going to run away. I didn't believe him. But I just noticed my camera was missing, and I wondered — " He looked at Terry as though she could help him.

"We'd better look for him," Terry said.

The boys and Terry took out their bikes and they all went off to search, with Danny and Mr. O'Halloran walking. The others seemed to be covering every direction except toward the river, so Terry went that way.

When she came to the place where they climbed down the bank, it occurred to her that Soupy might have been mad enough to come here. He knew he wasn't supposed to. Good grief, she hoped he wouldn't think of trying to climb under the bridge again.

"Soupy, are you down there?" she called.

Silence. He might be too angry to answer. She hated to climb down by herself, but it was the only way to make sure.

Sliding carefully down the bank, she could hear the pebbles rattling underfoot in the spooky quiet.

Then she saw him, sitting by the inlet with his feet in the water, his shoes beside him.

"Lemme be," he told Terry without turning.

Terry sat down beside him. She saw with relief that he had his father's camera cradled carefully in his arms.

"Why did you take the camera?" she asked.

"I'm going to throw it in the river," Soupy said, his voice quavering.

Terry put an arm around his shoulders but he shook it off. "You aren't either," she told him. "It's worth hundreds of dollars and your father would feel terrible if anything happened to it."

"I don't care," Soupy said shakily. "Anyhow I'm going in swimming."

"No, you're not. Don't even talk about swimming in the river," Terry said. "You're going to tell me why you were so mad at me yesterday."

Soupy hunched over so she couldn't see his face. "Can't," he mumbled. "Not spose to remine people when you have a — " He couldn't finish.

Terry remembered his saying something like that once before. It had been funny then. Yes, it was on her birthday. He wanted to make sure she knew his birthday was coming.

"Oh, no!" she cried. "I missed your birthday. It must have been last week." How could she have forgotten? She'd been so busy riding her bike and the time had flown by.

"Soupy, that was a terrible thing for me to do. But I didn't mean to. I'd give anything if I hadn't," she said earnestly.

Soupy went on sobbing.

"You should be mad at me. You got a right," Terry said. It would be different if he had forgotten hers. But she should know better. She remembered how he had appeared at her door on her birthday before she was even awake. And she had been too selfish to keep track of his. This was one time when something that happened was her fault.

Now she was crying too.

Presently Soupy said, "I wasn't really going to throw the camera in the river. I wasn't going swimming neither."

"I know," Terry said. She breathed a sigh of relief. He wasn't mad at her anymore. "I hope you aren't going to run away every time you get mad at somebody," she told him. "You scare everybody when you do that."

"My mother runned away," Soupy said, his voice shaking again. This time he let her put her arm around him.

"How did you find out? Did your father tell you?" Terry asked incredulously.

"I heard Mike and Danny talking about it. I don't think Daddy knows," Soupy said.

Why on earth hadn't Soupy told her sooner? He always came to her with his troubles. Suddenly she knew why. She hadn't been around. After all the years they'd been friends, she had deserted him. The same thing she had done to Cindy. But worse. Cindy could get along without her, but Soupy needed her.

Soupy was looking at her reproachfully. "Did you know allatime?" he asked.

Terry was trying to think of an answer when Mr. O'Halloran joined them.

"I saw your bike and knew you had to be around somewhere," he said to her.

He scooped Soupy up and hugged him. "You crazy kid," he said. "What are you trying to do to me? You want to turn me into an old man?"

Soupy squirmed happily in his father's arms. "You're old now," he said, giggling.

Terry told Mr. O'Halloran that the camera was all right.

"Camera?" he said. "Oh, yes. I'll take it now."

Soupy handed it over and they scrambled up the bank.

At the apartment Mr. O'Halloran went in. Terry told him she would let the others know Soupy was found.

She threw back her head and screamed at the top of her lungs, *"Oley, oley, olson, freedom!"* If it brought them in from hide and seek, it should bring them home now. From far away she heard an answering shout.

Terry and Soupy sat down on the front step to wait. There was something Terry had long ago decided to do after Soupy's birthday. What was it?

"Your library card — as soon as you can write your whole name, you can get your own card, now that you're six. And I'll teach you to write your last name," she said enthusiastically.

She waited for Soupy to get excited.

"I can't go that far by myself," Soupy said.

"I'll take you," Terry said. A long time ago she had promised to take him to the library and she hadn't gotten around to it yet. Maybe Soupy didn't believe her. "I'll take you tomorrow. And you can take your own books out."

"I can't read," Soupy pointed out.

"All right! I'll read them to you. Pretty soon school starts and you'll be learning to read by yourself," she said.

"Not me," Soupy replied. "I'd rather have you read to me."

She could picture his telling the first-grade teacher that. He would too.

As soon as the boys returned, they wanted to resume their football game. "We could have played a couple of games by now if it wasn't for that goop," Danny said, glaring at Soupy.

"He's just a baby. Forget it," Mike said.

Soupy studied the tips of his shoes. His face didn't change expression. But he glanced suddenly at Terry and away again. He really minded what his brothers said, Terry thought. It had never occurred to her before.

"He isn't a baby either," she said shrilly. "And you guys don't have to yell at him all the time. Who do you think you are? What did he ever do to you that you have to pick on him every minute? He's got just as much right to live as you do."

141

Mike and Danny backed away as she advanced toward them.

Mike, putting his hands up defensively, said, "Hold it, take it easy. We're not trying to murder him. C'mon, let's play football."

Terry seized her advantage with a sudden inspiration. Soupy was always on the side lines as far as the boys were concerned — even more than she was. Yet he was a boy, and not a baby anymore. It was time they stopped treating him like a baby. She demanded that Soupy be allowed to be the center after this.

The boys didn't like it. But they were startled and didn't want another outburst. The best objection Danny could muster was, "He doesn't even know how."

"I'll teach him," Terry said firmly. "C'mon, Soup."

Soupy looked to the right of him. He looked to the left. Then, still unbelieving, he stood up and followed her out to the street.

Tommy and Danny lined up by one street light, Mike and Greg by the next. That was their playing field.

After Terry flipped a coin to see who would get the kickoff, Greg punted. Danny caught the ball and ran, but he didn't get far before he was tagged. Then Terry showed Soupy how to be a center.

"Bend way down," she said. "Look between your legs. You have to throw the ball to whoever's closest — Look out!"

She caught him just in time. "You're not supposed

to fall over. Now try to keep your balance," she directed.

Terry threw the ball to Tommy and ran out of the way. Soupy stayed, and he and Tommy did a little dance while Mike and Greg came forward. Danny pulled Soupy away just as Tommy threw a desperate lateral pass. Terry was the only one around to receive it. Well, she was playing, wasn't she?

She caught it. Facing her were both teams. Behind her was a clear field. She turned and ran to the goal line.

"Hey, what'dya think you're doing?" Greg asked.

"I made a touchdown," Terry said complacently. "The center's always in the game just as much as everybody else. You never let me carry the ball. Well, now I made a touchdown and you got yourselves a new center. If you're nice to him, that is. Otherwise maybe he won't play."

The boys were in a vise and they knew it. Terry was through being the center and Soupy would do whatever she told him.

"What's the problem?" Mike said. "She made a touchdown. That's six points for you and me, Greg."

"It is not," Tommy said. "Danny and I had the ball."

"So it's a safety," Greg said, grinning. "Only costs you two points."

Mrs. Seth called from the window for Terry to come upstairs. As Terry left, the boys were screaming at each other.

It was a wonderful finish to her football career. And Soupy would love being the center.

"I'm sorry to interrupt the game," her mother said. "But I think this is finished at last. I'd like you to try it on to make sure, so I can still work on it today if it isn't right."

She took a good look at Terry and said, startled, "What have you been doing? There's sand all over you. And your shoes are a mess. I thought you weren't going to get involved in the game. How could you get so dirty in touch football anyway?"

Terry looked down at her shoes. She had a vague memory of accidentally dangling them in the river when she was sitting by Soupy. The sand must be from the bank. Mrs. Seth reached out and pulled a twig from Terry's hair.

Her mother didn't seem to know about Soupy's running away. She'd better explain. She'd start by telling her mother she was through with football. That should please her.

"I made a touchdown," she began. As soon as the words were out, she realized it was a poor beginning.

"That's fine. That's just fine," her mother said wearily. "All this time I've spent, taking time from the things I should be doing, making you a dress that you will probably ruin the first time you wear it. And just when I thought you were beginning to act like a young lady."

It was too much for Terry, on top of the scare Soupy had given her.

"I don't want to wear it. I hate it!" she shrilled. She picked up the jumper with both hands, ready to throw it on the floor. There was a ripping sound between her hands.

Horrified, Terry stared at the jumper. It wasn't her fault, she hadn't meant to tear it. Yes, it was too her fault. If she hadn't handled it so roughly, it wouldn't have torn.

She was hateful, a mean hateful person. She hated herself. Any punishment her mother gave her for tearing the jumper would be too little.

Mrs. Seth gently took the jumper from her. "Please, Terry, don't stand there like a statue. Sit down," she said. "I've been scolding you ever since you came in, haven't I? Why should you stay perfectly clean when you play? I want you to have fun, more fun than I had as a child. When I was your age, I was always neat. But it isn't all that important. You know, when I was working overtime and saw how hard you were trying to help, I made a resolve not to scold you so much. It seemed like I was doing it all the time. But I get so tired sometimes, with so much on my mind, and there never seems time to stop and think — "

Terry's mind was in a whirl. Her mother was trying to take the blame. It wasn't right.

"But I tore it," she insisted. "After all the work you did on it. And I was mean to Soupy — " In a rush

Terry told her mother about Soupy's birthday and his running away and that Soupy had found out about his mother, and she, Terry, hadn't been around to help him.

"But after this, I'm going to be more like Tommy. You'll see," Terry finished. "I know why you like him better and — "

"Stop!" her mother cried. "How can anyone get things so mixed up? I don't like Tommy better. And I don't want you to be just like him. You're not identical twins so why should you be alike? Your main trouble is that you're too impulsive, Terry. You don't stop to think before you act."

"Let me finish," she said as Terry started to speak. "But you're just as impulsive about good things as bad. You make me so angry sometimes, but just as often I'm proud of you. Only I never get around to telling you so."

Terry was having a hard time taking all this in, but she was relieved already to know her mother didn't find her so terrible.

Mrs. Seth was studying the jumper.

"Can it be fixed?" Terry asked hopefully.

Her mother held it up to inspect it closer. She burst out laughing. "Isn't that awful? I didn't sew up that seam, it was only basted. But I'm glad it happened. It gave us a chance to talk things out."

Terry's mother said she would repair the damage later. Right now she wanted to let Mr. O'Halloran know that Soupy had found out about his mother.

Terry went outside to watch the football game.

Soupy was bending over, trying to throw the ball. He couldn't let it go. Finally it sailed out of his hands, high in the air, and Greg had to jump for it. But Tommy and Danny waited until he caught it before they went for him. Soupy was working out all right. He'd learn.

She leaned against the building and sighed with satisfaction. Everything was fine. Her mother was proud of her.

Suddenly she straightened up. Why was her mother proud of her? What had she done right lately?

In future her mother would have reason to be proud of her, Terry decided. She had an idea.

Young Lady at Last?

TERRY GOT OFF to an early start the next morning. She had a lot to do. First she had to teach Soupy to write his last name so he could get his library card. Then she had to do some research at the library. And she was going to wear her new dress all day.

She had had an awful time getting permission to wear the dress. She wanted to prove to her mother that she could wear it and keep it clean for a whole day as the first step in being a young lady.

"But I don't *want* you to be a young lady," her mother kept saying. "I only say that when you aggravate me. Sometimes I forget how young you are. What I really want is for you to be yourself. Don't you ever say things you don't mean?"

"Well, I do things I don't mean all the time," Terry had replied. "But can't I just *try?*"

Finally her mother consented. "But don't go overboard on this, Terry," she said. "Something always happens when you do."

So Terry wore the dress. It was finished now, and it was beautiful. She felt like a different person in it. Older, and more in command of things. And she was going to be what her mother always said she wanted her to be. A young lady. Maybe her mother had changed her mind, but she couldn't have been wrong all that time. It just wasn't right. Her mother was going to have what she wanted even if she didn't want it.

But first off she had a promise to make up to Soupy. He was going to have his library card.

Reluctantly he wrote *Kevin* when she told him to, but he didn't approve. Finally she had an inspiration.

"Sure, Soupy is your name," she said. "But Kevin is your library name." He went along with that.

Then there was the job of teaching him to write his last name.

"I don't know why you had to have a name like O'Halloran," she complained.

She had him copy his name. She had him trace it at the window the way she had to trace maps for school. Then she made him write it without any help. It took all morning, but at last he seemed to be ready.

Soupy showed his first enthusiasm when they entered the library. He ran around pulling out books. She made him put them back.

"Wait till we get your card," she whispered.

At the desk, Miss Goodhue gave Soupy a form on which to write his name. He looked at it blankly.

"Go ahead," Terry urged him.

"I don't remember," Soupy said mournfully.

"He knows how," Terry said. "Honest. He did it at home."

Miss Goodhue showed Soupy a statement on the form. It said that he would agree to take care of the books he took out and that he knew the rules of the library.

"Can you read this?" Miss Goodhue asked him.

Soupy stared at her.

"But he's six. And he does know how to write his name," Terry protested. "And I promised him he could have a library card."

"Wasn't that promising something that wasn't up to you?" Miss Goodhue pointed out.

"But I thought — " Terry began.

"It's O.K.," Soupy said. "It don't matter, Terry. You take me out a book on your card."

"What is his name?" the librarian asked Terry.

Terry spelled it out for her and she wrote it down on a piece of paper.

"All right, young man, can you copy this?" Miss Goodhue asked.

Soupy copied it, somewhat illegibly. Miss Good-

hue made out a card for him and told him to write his name on it and to have his parents sign it.

"Gee, thanks," Terry said.

"I'd hate to disappoint such a steady customer," Miss Goodhue told her. "And I'm sure you will show your friend how to take care of his books. But try not to make rash promises after this."

"I won't," Terry said.

She and Soupy tore home and had Mr. O'Halloran sign the card. Then they hurried back to the library.

Soupy planted himself in front of the picture books and started pulling them out right and left. " 'N I want Pooh Bear, too," he demanded. "Where's Pooh Bear?"

Terry helped him take all his books to a table.

"You sit here and pick out three books and I'll get Pooh," she whispered. She went over to the shelf and found *Winnie-the-Pooh*.

Now she could do her research. The trouble with being a young lady was she didn't have the least idea how. But whenever Tommy didn't know how to do something, he looked it up in a book. He said everything was in books and all you had to do was find the right one. And the way to find the right one was to look it up in the card catalog. Her mother would be proud of her now, Terry thought. She was really thinking.

Terry checked under Y for Young Lady. Nothing. There must be another name for it.

Charm, that was it. She looked in the C drawer. No

Charm. Frustrated, she tried to think of some way other than asking Miss Goodhue. It was an embarrassing sort of thing to ask for.

Just then Soupy came bounding over. "Look what I found. I got Ferdinan' and the man that made up lions and Murbelly Street," he exclaimed.

"That's Mulberry Street, and quiet down," Terry hissed. "I read you all those books already. Why don't you find some new ones?"

"But I like these," Soupy said dolefully. He started away, muttering, "What good is a liberary card if you can't have the books you want?"

Terry drew him back. "O.K., you can take out those books. Listen, Soup, you want to do me a favor?"

Soupy nodded. Terry whispered his instructions and he strode purposefully over to the librarian's counter.

"Hey, you got any books on how to be a young lady?" Terry heard him yell. She dived between the stacks.

Honestly, if she didn't spell everything out for him, he made a complete hash of things. Why couldn't he use his head? That train of thought was painfully familiar. Well, she would have to teach Soupy to think before he acted, too.

Peeking around a corner, she saw Miss Goodhue guiding Soupy to a place in the nonfiction section.

Terry was planning to circle around to that spot

when Soupy shouted, "Here's the young lady books, Terry."

Mortified, Terry joined him. She could feel her ears burning. She didn't say a word to Soupy but he read the look in her eyes.

"What'd I do?" he asked. "You said you wanted — "

"Forget it, don't make it worse than it already is," Terry pleaded. Grabbing the first book that seemed likely, she rushed Soupy over to the counter to have the books checked out and then out of the building.

At least that was over. She wasn't sure now that thinking was all it was cracked up to be. But she'd see it through somehow.

Not wanting to waste the time spent in walking home, she decided to start learning right away how to be a young lady. She opened the book.

"Read it to me," Soupy said.

Terry flipped through the book and read out some of the headings. "The care of your feet." "Don't flash flashy jewelry around." "Liquids to your right, salads to your left." "The telephone is for the whole family."

She had to raise her voice as a truck, wetting the street, squished around the corner in front of them. "A basic color for your wardrobe," she read out loudly. Being a young lady was going to be harder than she thought.

Just as she reached the curb, she squealed, "Do you let a boy kiss you on the first date?" and toppled over into the soaked street.

She managed to save the book, but the bottom of the dress and jumper were a muddy mess. Now what on earth was she going to do?

"Well, do you?" Soupy asked curiously when he saw she wasn't hurt.

"Do I what?" she asked crossly.

"Let a boy kiss you on the first date," he said.

"Nobody better try it," she snapped. "Listen, Soupy, maybe you'd better go home and look at your books. I'm going over to Cindy's and see if she can think of something to do about the dress, and I don't know how long I'll be." She figured she could think better without him.

He left when she promised to read his books to him just as soon as possible.

Cindy and her mother were both sympathetic when Terry explained she had promised to keep the dress clean all day. Mrs. Ford said they could use the washing machine since Cindy knew how.

"But let me know when you are ready for the dryer," she said. "It's still new and I'm not quite used to it yet myself."

Cindy gave Terry jeans and a blouse to put on until her clothes were ready. Before Cindy could stop her, Terry had poured a lot of soap into the machine so the mud would be sure to come out.

"Too much soap isn't good for the machine," Cindy said.

They watched with worried eyes as frothy bubbles piled out of the top of the machine.

"Think," Terry told herself. Too much soap? Simple.

"I'll let some of it out," she said, opening the door a little. But the water wasn't about to come out a little at a time. It whooshed out, and the machine stopped automatically. They had to get Mrs. Ford to start it again.

Cindy's mother didn't scold them. She just informed Cindy that the mop was where it was always kept.

"It was my fault," Terry said. She was about to add that she hadn't meant to do it, when she thought better of it. Yesterday she had decided that wasn't any excuse.

"A scrubbing won't hurt this floor," Mrs. Ford said. "Don't look so sad, Terry. Nothing terrible happened."

Terry insisted on doing all the mopping up. While she worked, she tried to figure out what had happened. She had been thinking when she decided to open the door. But she hadn't thought about what might happen afterwards. That was it. Thinking, but not thinking long enough. She wondered if she would ever learn how to do it. But she was determined to go on trying.

Cindy's mother put the dress and jumper in the dryer and then she ironed them. Terry was getting anxious. Her mother must be home by now.

Just when her clothes were ready, it started to pour

outside. "What good is thinking when something like this happens," Terry moaned.

"What?" Cindy asked.

"Nothing," Terry said. It was too hard to explain.

She was invited to stay and eat, but she wanted to get home. Yet she didn't want to get her dress wet in the rain.

"You wear my things," Cindy said. "I'll get you a plastic bag for your clothes and the book."

Terry thanked Cindy and her mother and was on her way before Mrs. Ford had a chance to suggest she take an umbrella.

Changing quickly in the shower room down the hall, Terry stuffed the jeans and blouse in the bag and stole quietly into her apartment. She put the bag behind the sofa and went into the other room where her mother had already started supper.

"Hi," Terry said. "How does the dress look now?"

Her mother jumped. "Goodness, I didn't even hear you come in," she said.

She looked from Terry's clean dress to her wet hair and her muddy shoes and socks. Terry felt her hair and looked down at her feet. She could see it was of no use.

She set the table while she told her mother about her miserable day. "I just can't do anything right," she said. "I don't know why you should ever be proud of me. Everything I do comes out wrong."

"Didn't you go through all that in trying to do something to please me?" her mother asked. "I'm proud of you for that."

"But it didn't work out right," Terry said.

"The dress looks all right to me, although I'm sorry you felt you had to go through all that for it," her mother said. "And who ever told you it was your job to take care of Soupy?"

"Well, nobody," Terry said.

"When I was your age, I was helping take care of my younger brothers and sisters," her mother said. "I had to. I was the oldest. It was my responsibility. But no one ever said Soupy was your responsibility. And yet ever since he could toddle, you've been looking out for him. I told Mr. O'Halloran once what a shame it was that Soupy didn't have his mother here in the years when a mother is most important. And he said that was true, but his son was awfully lucky to have a friend like you. I've always been very proud of you for that, Terry. When I think of more reasons, I'll let you know."

Terry was feeling better and better. She decided to ask her mother something she'd been wondering about for a long time.

"How could Soupy's mother go off like that and never come back? Wouldn't you think she'd see what a terrible thing she'd done and want to come back?"

"I'd think so," her mother said. "But sometimes

when people make such a big mistake, they're too ashamed to do anything about it afterward. I'm not saying that's what happened, but it could be."

"Oh," Terry said.

"Don't you ever get like that," her mother said sternly. "When you make a mistake, face up to it." She paused, looking startled. "What am I scolding you for?" she said. "You haven't done anything. And as for this business of being a young lady, don't worry about it. The most important qualities you already have. Let the rest come when it will. Now go get your brother. I think he's at the O'Hallorans."

Terry laughed and ran. She told Tommy to come and eat and assured Soupy that she would come and read to him after supper.

As they went down the hall, Tommy said, "What are you grinning about?"

"Me great thinker. Ugh," Terry said, pounding her chest.

"You're nuts," her brother said.

After supper, as she was drying the dishes, Terry was so full of joy that she burst into song. Her mother joined in. Tommy stared at them for a minute and then added his voice. As he sang, he put the dishes away, any place he found room.

Terry waited for her mother to tell him to do it right, but Mrs. Seth said nothing. Terry thought, "If I did that —" and looked at her mother.

Her mother smiled and shrugged as if to say, "If you were doing it, I know you would put them in the right place."

"So who cares where the silly old dishes go," Terry grinned back.

They went on singing, each a little off key, but together they made a cheerful sound.

THE END